BLIND SIGHT

Book One

Lucille Pfiffer Mystery Series

Tanya R. Taylor

Tanya R. Taylor is a Readers' Favorite Award Winning Author. She has been writing ever since she was a child and published her first book titled: *A Killing Rage* as a young adult. She is now the author of both fiction and non-fiction literature. Her books have made Amazon Kindle's Top 100 Paid Best-sellers' List in several categories. Tanya writes in various genres including: Paranormal Romance, Fantasy, Thrillers, Science fiction, Mystery and Suspense.

Her book ***Cornelius***, the first installment in a successful series, climbed to number one **in Amazon's Teen & Young-adult Multi-generational Family Fiction** category. And ***INFESTATION: A Small Town Nightmare*** and ***CARA*** are both number one **international** bestsellers.

Never Miss a New Release by
Tanya R. Taylor!

Sign up at
Tanya-r-taylor.com

GET BOOK TWO IN THIS EXCITING, NEW COZY MYSTERY SERIES!

1

Super Vanilla

I carefully descended the air-conditioned jitney and started down the sidewalk with my cane in hand and Nilla, my pet Shih Tzu on leash at my side. Taking a cab was our preferred mode of transport, but sometimes we enjoyed a nice, long bus ride instead. Nestled on both sides of the street were a number of shops, including convenience stores, jewelry, liquor, antique stores and haberdashery.

It was the day before my scheduled meeting with the local pet society that, while walking along downtown Chadsworth, I heard a woman scream. The vision of her anguished face flashed into my mind and the image of a young boy dressed in faded blue jeans and a long-sleeved black shirt running at full speed in the direction Nilla and I were headed. Gripped tightly in his hand was a purse that did not belong to him; his eyes bore a mixture of confidence in his escape intertwined with fear of capture. He was quickly approaching—now only several feet behind us. In no time, he would turn the bend just ahead and be long gone bearing the ill-gotten fruits of his labor.

One could imagine how many times he'd done the same thing and gotten away with it, only to plan his next move – to stealthily lie in wait for his unsuspecting victim. I heard the squish-squashing of his tennis shoes closely behind. It was the precise moment he was about to zoom past us that I abruptly held out my cane to the left, tripping him, and watched as he fell forward, rolling over like a car tire, then ultimately landing flat on his back on the hard pavement. I dropped the leash and yelled, "Get him, Nilla!"

Nilla took off at full speed and pounced on top of the already injured boy, biting him on every spot she could manage – determined to teach him a lesson he'd never forget. He screamed and tried to push her off of him, but a man dashed over and pinned him to the ground. I made my way over to Nilla and managed to get her away from the chaotic scene. Her job was done. As tiny as she was, she made her Momma proud.

The frantic woman got her purse back and the boy was restrained until police arrived.

2

The room was almost packed to capacity when I arrived at the podium with the gracious assistance of a young man. As he went to take his seat in the front row, I proceeded with my introduction: “My name’s Lucille Pfiffer—Mrs., that is—even though my husband Donnie has been dead and gone for the past four and a half years now. We had no children, other than our little Shih Tzu, Vanilla; ‘Nilla’ for short.” I smiled, reflectively. “By the way, I must tell you she doesn’t respond to ‘Nill’ or ‘Nillie’; it’s ‘Nilla’ if you stand a chance of getting her attention. She totally ignores you sometimes even when you call her by her legal name ‘*Va (vuh)*…nilla’.

“We reside in a quiet part of town known as Harriet’s Cove. A little neighborhood with homes and properties of all sizes. We’re mostly middle class folk, pretending to be upper class. The ones with large homes, much bigger than my split level, are the ones you hardly see strolling around the neighborhood, and they certainly don't let their kids play with yours if you've got any. Those kids are the 'sheltered' ones—they stay indoors mainly, other than when it's time to hop in the family car and go wherever for whatever."

I heard the rattle inside someone's throat.

"Uh, Mrs. Pfiffer…" A gentleman at the back of the room stood up. "I don't mean to be rude or anything, but you mentioned the neighbors' kids as if you can see these things you described going on in your neighborhood. I mean, how you said some don't play with others and they only come out when they're about to leave the house. But how do you know any of this? Or should we assume, it's by hearsay?"

I admired his audacity to interrupt an old lady while she's offering a requested and well-meaning introduction to herself. After all, I was a newbie to the Pichton Pet Society and their reputation for having some 'snobby' members preceded them.

"Thank you very much, sir, for the questions you raised," I answered. "Yes, you are to assume that I know some of this—just some—via hearsay. The rest I know from living in my neck of the woods for the past thirty-five years. I haven't always been blind, you know." I liked how they put you front and center on the little platform to give your introductory speech. That way, no eyes could miss you and you think, for one delusionary moment, that you're the cream of the crop. Made a woman my age feel really special. After all, at sixty-eight, three months and four days, and a little *over-the-hill*, I highly doubted there were going to be any young studs falling head over heels in love with me and showering me with their attention.

"Pardon me, ma'am." He gave a brief nod and sat back down again.

I took that as an apology. I could see the look on Merlene's face as she sat in the fourth row from the front. She thought I'd blown my cover for a minute there, but she keeps forgetting that I'm no amateur at protecting my interests. Sure, I sometimes talk a bit too much and gotta put my foot in my mouth afterwards, but my decades of existence gives me an excuse.

I could hear Merlene scolding me now:

"Lucille, I've told you time and time again, you must be careful of what you say! No one's gonna understand how an actual blind woman can see the way you do. They won't believe you even if you told them!"

Her words were like a scorched record playing in my brain. She got on my nerves with all her warnings, but I was surely glad I was able to drag her down there to the meeting with me that day.

I tried not to face that guy's direction anymore, even though the dark sunglasses I wore served its purpose of concealing my *blind stare.* "Thank you, sir," I said. "Well, I guess there's not much left to say about me, except that I used to have a career as a private banker for about twenty years. After that, I retired to spend more time with Donnie, who'd just retired from the Military a year earlier. We spent the next twenty-one years together until he passed away from heart trouble."

Someone else stood up—this time a lady around my age. "If you don't mind my asking…at what point did you lose your eyesight? And how are you possibly able to care for your pet Vanilla?"

When I revisit that part of my life, I tend to get a tad emotional. "It was a little over eight years ago that I developed a rare disease known as Simbalio Flonilia. I know, it sounds like a deadly virus or something, but it's a progressive and rather aggressive deterioration of the retina. They don't know what causes it, but within a year of my diagnosis, I was totally blind. I'm thankful for Donnie because after it happened, he kept me sane. Needless to say, I wasn't handling being blind so well after having been able to see all of my life. Donnie was truly a life-saver and so was Nilla. She's so smart—she gets me everything I need and she's very protective, despite her little size. I've cared for Nilla ever since she was two months old and I pretty much know where everything is regarding her. Taking care of her is the easy part. Her taking care of me is another story."

Though somewhat hazy, I could see the smiles on many of their faces. The talk of Nilla obviously softened some of their rugged features.

Mrs. Claire Fairweather, the chairperson, came and stood right next to me.

"Lucille, we are happy to welcome you as the newest member of our organization!" She spoke, eagerly. "You have obviously been a productive member of Chadsworth for many years and more importantly, you are a loving mom to your precious little dog, Vanilla. People, let's give her a warm round of applause!"

A gentleman came and helped me to my chair. The fragrance he was wearing reminded me of how much Donnie loved his cologne. Such a fine man, he was. If it were up to him, I wouldn't have worked a day of my married life. It would've been enough for him to see me every day at home just looking pretty and smiling. His engineering job paid well enough, but I loved my career and since it wasn't a stressful one, I didn't feel the need to quit to just sit home and do nothing.

"Thank you, dear," I told the nice, young man.

"My pleasure, Mrs. Pfiffer."

Merlene leaned in as Claire proceeded with the meeting. "I told you—you talk too blasted much!" She whispered. "If you keep up this nonsense, they're gonna take your prized disability checks away from you."

"It'll happen over my dead body, Merlene," I calmly replied.

"Mrs. Pfiffer, I must say it's truly an honor that you've decided to join us here at the Pichton Pet Society," Claire said at the podium. "With your experience as a professional, I'm sure you'll have lots of ideas on how we can raise funds for the continued care of senior pets, stray dogs and abused animals. Your contribution to this group would be greatly appreciated."

After the meeting, she'd caught Merlene and me at the door, as we were about to head for Merlene's Toyota.

"I'm so glad you joined us, Mrs. Pfiffer. My secretary will be in touch with you about our next meeting."

"Thank you, Mrs. Fairweather. I'm honored that you accepted me. After all, animals are most precious. Anything that supports their best interest, I'm fired up for."

"Did you always love animals?" she asked.

I gulped. "Well, if I may be straight with you… I hated them— especially dogs!"

Her hand flew to her chest and a scowl crept over her face. I must have startled her by the revelation.

"It was after Nilla came into our life that I soon found a deep love and appreciation for animals—especially dogs. To me, they're just like precious little children who depend on us adults to take care of them and to show them love, as I quickly learned that they have the biggest heart for their owners."

Fairweather seemed relieved and a wide smile stretched across her face. "Oh, that's so good to know! I was afraid there for a moment that we'd made a terrible mistake by accepting you into our organization!" She laughed it off.

I did a pretend laugh back at her. I may be blind, but I'm not stupid—that woman actually just insulted me to my face!

"I don't know why you want to be a part of that crummy group with those snooty, snobbish, high society creeps anyway!" Merlene remarked after we both got in the car.

I rested my cane beside me. "Because I've been a part of crummy groups for most of my adult life. I don't know anything different."

Merlene gave me a reprimanding look. "It's not funny, Lucille. You dragged me out here to sit with people who, I admit love animals, but they seem to hate humans! I've heard some things about that Fairweather woman that'll make your eyes roll. You know she's a professor at the state college, right?"

"Uh huh."

"Well, I heard she treats the kids who register for her class really badly. She fails most of them every single term. The only ones who pass are the ones who kiss up to her."

"If there's a high failure rate in her class, why would the state keep her on then?" I asked.

"Politics. She got there through politics and is pretty much untouchable. I heard she also was a tyrant to her step-kids. Pretty much ran them all out of the house and practically drove the second fool who married her insane. He actually ended up in the loony bin and when he died, she took everything—not giving his kids a drink of water they can say they'd inherited."

"I blame the husband for that."

"Not when she got him to sign over everything to her in his will when he wasn't in his right mind. The whole thing was contested, but because she was politically connected, she came out on top. After that, she moved on to husband number three. If I knew that woman was the chairperson of this meeting you dragged me out to, I would've waited in the car for you instead of sitting in the same room with her."

We were almost home when Merlene finally stopped talking about Fairweather. You'd think the woman didn't have a life of her own, considering the length of time she focused on this one individual she obviously couldn't stand. I just wanted to get the hell out of that hot car (the two front windows of which couldn't roll down), and get home to my Nilla. She'd be waiting near the door for me for sure.

I wish I was allowed to bring her to the meeting. They claimed they're all about animals, but not one was in that room. I guess I was being unfair since they mentioned that particular Monday meeting was the only one they couldn't bring their pets to. That was the meeting where new members were introduced and important plans for fundraisers were often discussed.

"I'll see you later, Lucille. Going home to do some laundry," Merlene said after pulling up onto my driveway. "Need help getting out?"

"I'm good," I replied.

"How sharp is it now?"

"I can see the outline of your face. Nothing else at the moment. Everything was almost crystal clear in the meeting."

"Yeah. Inopportune time for it to have been crystal clear," Merlene mumbled.

She was used to my *inner vision*, as we call it, going in and out like that. I grabbed hold of my cane and the tip of it hit the ground as I turned to get out of the vehicle. "I can manage just fine. I'm sure it'll come back when it feels like. Thanks for coming out with me."

I smiled as I thought of how much she often sacrificed for me. Ten years my junior, Merlene was a good friend. We had a row almost every day, but we loved one another. She and I were like the typical married couple.

"By the way, I forgot to mention, my tenant Theodore, told me this morning that someone had called about renting the last vacant room."

"Perfect!" Merlene said.

"Said he was coming by this afternoon. What time is it?"

"It's a quarter of five."

I had an idea. "Merlene, he's supposed to show up at five o'clock. You wanna hang around for a few minutes to see what my prospects are? Maybe he's tall, dark and handsome and I may stand a chance."

"I doubt it," she squawked. "Besides, I must get at least a load of laundry done today. If not, I'll likely have to double up tomorrow for as quick as that boy goes through clothes! I tell ya, ever since he met that Delilah, he's changed so much."

"Why don't you leave that boy alone?" I barked. "He's twenty-seven-years-old, for Heaven's sake! Allow him to date whomever the hell he feels like. He's gotta live and learn, you know, and buck his head when need be. You and I went through it and so must he. You surely didn't allow your folks to tell you who you ought to date and who you shouldn't, did you? And furthermore, why do you keep calling Juliet, *Delilah*?"

"Because she's just like that Delilah woman in the Bible; can't be trusted!" Merlene spoke her mind. "And since you asked—why do you call her *Juliet*? Her name's Sabrina."

I sighed. "You know why I call her that."

"I tell ya...she's no Juliet!"

"Anyway, you're gonna wait with me a few minutes while I interview this newcomer or not?" I'd just had enough of Merlene's bickering for one day.

I heard her roll up the two remaining car windows and pull her key out of the ignition. It was one among a ring of keys.

Nilla was right at the front door when I let myself in. I leaned down and scooped up my little princess. She licked my face and I could feel the soft vibration of her wagging tail. Merlene walked in behind me.

"Nilla pilla!" she said, as she plonked down on the sofa. "Why can't you assist Mommy here with her interview? After all, you've gotta live with the newbie too."

I heard Theodore's footsteps descending the staircase. His was a totally different vibration from Anthony's. Anthony's steps were softer like that of a woman's feet. I had a good look at him a few times and he definitely was *Mister Debonair*. And that desk job he had at the computer company suited him just fine. Theodore was different; he was more hardcore, a blue collar worker at the welding plant, pee sprinkling the toilet seat kinda guy. That was my biggest problem with him – he wasn't all that tidy, especially in the bathroom. But I hadn't kicked him out already because he's got good manners and sort of treats me like I'm his mother. Anthony mostly stays to himself and that's fine with me too.

After I'd sat down, Nilla wiggled constantly to get out of my arms. She didn't like "hands" as much as she preferred dashing all over the place, particularly when her energy level was high. I could tell that was the case at the moment, so I gently let her down on the tiled floor and immediately saw her sprinting through the wide hallway which led into the kitchen, then doubling back into the living room seconds later, and making her way under the sofa. Under there was her favorite spot in the entire house. Often, she stayed in her hut-like habitat for hours at a time.

"Good evening, ladies," Theodore said as he entered the living room. How did the meeting go?"

"It was horrible!" Merlene replied.

"It went fine, Theodore. Beautiful atmosphere; beautiful people," I said.

"She got her fifteen minutes of fame," Merlene snapped. "That's all she cares about. She should've invited *you* to waste a full two hours there instead of me."

Theodore laughed. "Well, I'll be heading out to work. See you later."

"Yeah, later," Merlene replied.

As Theodore opened the door, he met someone standing on the other side. "Oh, I'm sorry. Almost bumped into you," he said.

Theodore went his way and the person stepped inside.

"What're you doing here, David?" Merlene asked.

"I'm here to see Miss Lucille. I'm interested in renting the room."

I could sense Merlene's shock. After all, why would her son who lives with her come to rent a room from me?

3

David had an air of innocence about him; he'd always been that way. He was more on the slim side, had dark hair and a cute dimple in his left cheek. He looked a lot like Merlene; her genes were obviously just as strong as her personality. That runaway husband of hers, Roy Bostwick, hardly injected any looks into their only child. I always thought Merlene's failed relationship with Roy had embittered her from ever investing in any new relationships since he upped and left her for a younger woman shortly after she retired as a school secretary. She'd spent just about all of her retirement money on expensive "man toys" like that convertible she had to fight him for in court after he'd left. Merlene was just never the same after the divorce. She went through her house on a daily basis, constantly looking for something to clean, or came over to my place to shoot the breeze, if we didn't have plans for an outing. That's of course, when she wasn't busy prying into David's personal affairs and trying to live her life through him.

"What are you talking about, David?" She sat straight up, suddenly finding the energy it took to do mounds of laundry when she got home.

"Mom, if you don't mind, I need to speak with Miss Lucille. You and I can talk later, okay?"

Merlene was stunned. Knowing her, she was also seething inside after being *casually* handled by her son.

"Miss Lucille, I called this morning, but was told you were in the restroom. I heard you have a vacant room for rent and was wondering if I can have it." He spoke with the humility of a saint. The boy was just so good. If I had children, I'd want them to be like him.

"Well, David… I don't know. I think you'd better discuss this with your mother. I really don't want to be placed in a situation where I must choose between my friend and her son." Although, in my mind, I was leaning more towards the boy. Maybe he only needed a short reprieve at my house to clear his head. Didn't know how that would happen though since Merlene's here almost every other day.

"David, what you're asking of Lucille is foolish! You have a home. What on earth are you thinking?" Merlene was clearly concerned.

"Mom, I love you, but you've become overbearing," he replied. "I'm a grown man; I'm sick of you trying to run my life."

"David..." she tried to interject, but he stopped her.

"Now, this thing with you and Sabrina has gone too far. If you don't think she's the right one for me, it's my job to find that out, but I'm not leaving home because of that situation. It's because of everything."

He glanced at me, then shifted his focus back to Merlene.

"I didn't want to do this in front of anyone, but Miss Lucille's like family." He paused for a moment. "What I'd planned to do was to move out completely and get myself an apartment, but decided instead to just take a little break and clear my head."

I was right on.

"Maybe after a while, I'll be back home, but things would have to change or I'm going back to plan A which is to get an apartment and leave for good."

I sensed Merlene was humbled by David's assertion and his poignant, yet subtle threat. I knew her greatest fear in life was losing him – and that would be in any way, shape or form. Moving out for good because she'd chased him off by dominance was worse than him deciding it was time to just venture out on his own. It seemed like a good ten years before she responded. It probably was the very first time I'd noticed my friend at a loss for words.

"Well, David… if that's how you feel. I mean… if being here is what you think you need, I won't try to stop you," she finally uttered, almost in a whisper.

My heart went out to her, but she knew she'd always see the boy because my house was just like her second home. I kind of wondered at first why David chose to come here instead of staying somewhere else for a while. He must have known by making such a move, he wasn't really getting away from his mother. Then it hit me that he was just trying to prove a point to her – to use this step as a warning so that he didn't have to do the thing she dreaded most which was to leave permanently. Smart kid. A kind one too.

"So, can I rent the room, Miss Lucille?" he asked.

I sighed deeply. "Seems fine with your mother; so the answer, my son, is yes. You can have the room for as long as you like."

"Great!"

"Now, bear in mind, there are rules. There'll be no drinking alcohol or smoking in my house; no shacking up in any of these bedrooms with any women – or men for that matter." I got the stare of shock when I said that, but I didn't care. He had to be told the rules just like all the others who'd rented rooms in my house. "The TV room, living room and front porch can be used for privacy when visitors come over. Everyone here can use the kitchen, but must each buy their own food and clean up their own mess. This is not a bed and breakfast, ya hear?

"I hear you, ma'am," he replied with a chuckle.

"That's good. And one other thing… no peeing on the toilet seat. You boys need to learn how to aim straight. As a cautionary method, please raise the seat. There'll be no special treatment because of your mother. You must obey the rules like everyone else." I raised my chin. "So, if the laws I've set down don't sit well with you, it would be best to walk right out of that door with your mother."

"Understood," he said. "When can I move in?"

"Anytime you're ready, sonny."

David went out and grabbed a large luggage bag from the trunk of his car. Merlene and I were surprised he'd wasted no time packing up his things and tagging them along.

I showed him to his room while Merlene waited downstairs. David stayed long enough to unpack his bag and then he was gone. Said he'd return in a couple of hours. We figured he'd gone to spend some time with Juliet.

"Can you believe that kid?" Merlene exclaimed.

I shook my head. "I told you, Merlene. You were gonna drive that boy away. I just never imagined he'd end up in my direction. No need to worry though; I'll keep a good eye on him."

"There you go joking again when we're discussing a serious matter, Lucille! My son just walked out on me and to *you*—my best friend! I'm so ashamed right now, I don't know what to do with myself."

"You can't be serious with that!" I grinned.

"What?"

I knew she was even more annoyed. "You said you're so ashamed!"

"That's right!"

"Well, it's not like he set you straight in front of strangers. Like he said, we're all practically family. You've never one day been ashamed of anything that happened in my presence. You're just making the matter seem far worse than it is."

Merlene was quiet for a few moments, perhaps pondering my assertion. "I guess you're right."

"The boy didn't disrespect you, my friend. He did what he did out of love because he doesn't want your relationship to be destroyed for good. Give the young man his space—which means don't go and *up* your visits here just to be checking on him. When he sees you're being mature about the whole thing, he'll be outta here and back with Momma in no time," I said.

4

"Ouuuuchhh!" I heard Theodore yell the next morning. Immediately, I knew who the culprit was. After slipping into my duster, I headed for the hallway. I'd just rolled over in bed a few minutes earlier after my six-thirty alarm buzzed, so wasn't quite in the mood for another of Nilla's disturbances.

My inner vision wasn't quite clear at that point, and though I knew my way around the house—every single inch of it—I was cautious to hold on to a wall here and there in case something was in the pathway. I was thankful for the occasional gift of sight without the use of my eyes, though sometimes faces and shapes were not clearly defined. I wondered why that was, but never once complained about it. To me, it was a rarely-given second chance.

"Theodore! What happened?" I asked as I walked along. "Where are you?"

"In my room. It's just Nilla again," he said, evenly.

I arrived at his bedroom and leaned against the door frame. "I figured as much! Nilla, dear. You mustn't be so mischievous. You know Theodore absolutely hates when you bite his toes!" The pitter-patter of my dog's little paws headed my way. I leaned over at just the right moment and picked her up. She hastily licked my face.

"There…there. Such a precious little princess you are. Be good, so you'll get an extra special treat today, okay? No more biting Theodore."

More licking.

My blank gaze went Theodore's way. "It *was* the toes again, wasn't it?"

"Yep, but I'm fine. My yell this time, unlike the other times, seemed to have gotten her attention. She actually stopped biting. Would you believe that?"

Theodore was always good about it, despite the numerous times Nilla yearned for a taste of those white socks he wore, then would afterwards sink her little teeth into Theodore's flesh. Thankfully, he always managed to prevent her from biting deep enough to cause any real harm.

"Guess she's finally learning now." I smiled. "So, are you off today?"

"I wish. I don't have to work the morning shift, so at least I get to stay in for a few hours and catch up on some rest."

"Well, I'm going to get her out of your hair and take her for an early walk, then we'll head into town. There's nothing like the fresh morning air."

First things first—I had to feed Nilla and at least grab a coffee for myself. Our walks often lasted around an hour.

Theodore's stare bore into the pit of my back as I descended the stairs with Nilla at my heel. I had my cane, but he just dreaded the ever-so-slight possibility that I could miss a step and go tumbling forward, perhaps, to eternity.

"I'm fine, Theodore," I calmly assured him. "I told you I know these steps like the back of my hand. Go back to bed. We both agree you need your rest."

I heard him leave, quietly. I'm sure he wanted me to think he was never there. They say that a blind person's sense of hearing is quite sharp. I'd have to agree. Before I lost my eyesight, people would sometimes have to repeat what they'd said to me, especially if they were several feet away. However, I found that I can hear the slightest sounds now, even Theodore there tip-toeing away. Then again, his steps were heavy anyway, so I'm not sure if a sharper sense of hearing can be attributed in this regard.

I always wore my sunglasses whenever I ventured outdoors. They certainly weren't to protect my eyes from the sun's rays, but simply to make a point to the general population to be careful when driving in close proximity to this old lady. And whenever Nilla's with me, they'd better be better extra careful.

She had on her favorite leather leash with the gold trimming. Merlene once asked me why I didn't get a guide dog, but I wondered if Nilla had suddenly become invisible to her. Sure, she was a little Shih Tzu, but she'd been with me before I ever went blind and no one knew or in my mind, could guide me better. She did wonderfully when I really needed her and no other dog could do any better.

The sun embraced me the moment I stepped out of the house and the crisp air flowing from the surrounding trees made my lungs happy. I heard birds chirping an indecipherable melody, but all I could see before me was darkness. It surrounded and blatantly reminded me of the dismal truth that I was, in fact, blind. The probing cane always came in handy in times like these. At least, I hadn't tripped over anything for a really long time, especially since at my age, a fall could be detrimental—it could mean a hip fracture or worse.

I knew which direction to turn from my front door and exactly where to go; that's the benefit of having lived in a neighborhood for many years. I hadn't always been brave enough to venture outside though. I remember those early days how terrified I was to go anywhere alone. It was hard enough depending on my loving Donnie for everything; just hated putting him through that. "In sickness and in health," he reminded me when need be. It was one of our vows which we both took very seriously.

I was sure by the distance Nilla and I had walked that we were passing Chloe Dunbar's house. Her home was at least four properties down from mine. Chloe was around my age and had pretty much ignored Donnie and me ever since she moved there ten years after we did. Heard she hadn't been doing so well for the past few years and was confined to a wheelchair. She often complained of seeing ghosts outside her windows every night after the care-taker put her to bed. By all accounts, even when the curtains were drawn, she still saw their silhouettes through the blackness of night, just as clear as day. No one took her seriously; they all thought she was nuts, but even though I'd never told her, I knew she was telling the truth. Sad state to be in when you see those apparitions and can't get away—when your bed becomes your nightly prison.

"Ruff!" Nilla barked.

"What's wrong, dear?" I asked, as she jerked a bit from my grip. I then heard the other barking, which meant we were passing Robert and Diane Clover's residence.

"Hi, Lucille! Hi, Nilla!" Diane's soft voice reached us moments later.

She tried to settle her two Pit Bulls behind the gate, but they were paying her no mind. I raised my hand. "Hey There!"

"How is everything?" Diane asked.

"Splendid. Just splendid!" I replied. "We're out for our usual walk."

"That's nice. Well, have fun, then. Bye, Nilla!" She waved.

Our neighborhood had always been well-kept. Everyone did their part to ensure their surroundings were kept neat and tidy. No stray dogs, as far as I knew, ran the streets and everyone's pets were either kept inside or enclosed by a fence or a gate. Sometimes, I got to see colorful flowers, the manicured lawns, and gorgeous greenery. I wish I was able to see them all the time during our walks, but I'm grateful for whenever I did.

Nilla and I continued on toward the cul-de-sac, which was an excellent guide for me, especially on days like this, as it took me straight around and finding home again was a breeze. We rarely ever ventured around the corner to the other section of the neighborhood where the properties were slightly elevated. They offered an attractive view into the subdivision from the main road.

As we approached the cul-de-sac, random images began to appear before me, then I realized after the mental ocean was calm that I could right then and there see Sir Clement Tucker's house—the one directly on the curb. Back in the day, Sir Clement was a wealthy British entrepreneur who'd migrated to Chadsworth with loads of his hard-earned money. He'd come to enjoy the warmer temperatures, but mainly to avoid paying taxes back in his hometown. Always keen on real estate, he sought to invest in large parcels of land throughout the city and within three years, owned the largest chunk of it, apart from the government. Harriet's Cove—my neighborhood—was his pride and joy.

A door slammed in the house. As far as I knew, that house had been vacant for most of the year as the grand-nephew and new owner, Luke Tucker, spent the past six months in England. The poor fellow always lamented to the local media how unfair it was that his grand-uncle had invested his money in that huge tract of land and some crookery went on in the legal system which transferred title of the remaining plots to big, bad Tony Brawn—the sharpest realtor to hit Chadsworth since Sir Clement's arrival. Luke's assertions had all fallen on deaf ears, however, and he and his family were convinced there was a conspiracy involving higher powers.

I gripped Nilla's leash a little tightly and decided to move on, when suddenly, there was a clashing sound coming from inside of the large house and within seconds, at least a dozen crows appeared on the front lawn. I hated when I saw those birds—feeling each time it was nothing more than a bad omen.

The house was quiet again.

Maybe Luke's back, I thought. *And maybe he's just having a hard day.*

I heard he'd had a lot of them since Sir Clement's passing. After all, who could blame him for feeling the way he felt, especially after his relative had contributed so much of his wealth to the betterment of this society? And far worse was the fact that Sir Clement's murder had never been solved—and according to the Tucker family—never properly investigated, for whatever reasons.

Nilla was becoming impatient. She'd started barking at the crows and edging closer to the gate. Despite her small frame, she was no coward. She'd take on anyone or anything regardless of their size or stature. She probably thought she'd have an advantage over the birds, but little did she know, those beaks of theirs could send her to the vet or an early grave in a matter of minutes. I gently pulled her along and we moved on.

Not only could I feel the sun, but without glancing up, I was able to see it. Having inner vision certainly came with its advantages. No worries about the sun glaring down at you if you made the mistake of looking up directly at it. The only problem was not knowing how long my inner vision would last. It came and went without warning.

A car slowed to the side of us. It was Carla Walkes and her girl, Brittany.

"Mornin', Lucille!" Carla said.

I tried not to immediately look in her direction. I believe Merlene had me a bit overly paranoid about this whole thing.

"Who's there?" I asked, knowingly.

"It's Carla. Can I give you and Nilla a lift into town or are you just having your morning stroll?"

Carla was kind enough to offer us a lift into town several times. She usually set out early to take Brittany for gymnastics practice. The fifteen-year-old was growing well and had been doing gymnastics since she was five.

"How nice of you, Carla! I'd planned to take a cab into town since I do have some shopping to do, but if you'd be so kind to give us a lift, we'd just take one back."

"Wonderful!" she exclaimed.

Brittany offered the front passenger seat to me and she gladly sat with Nilla in the back.

Carla was a big woman who took up most of the space between her driver's seat and the steering wheel. Yet, she had an attractive face and her size did no damage to her self-confidence, and rightfully so. I always thought, if only she could shave off about a hundred pounds, she'd look like a beauty queen. But so much for wishful thinking—it was no secret that Carla really loved to eat. She once told me she went on binges for nearly every emotional state she found herself in: whether she was happy, sad or angry—you name it. Thankfully, Brittany was on the thin side. Her dad's genes were probably much stronger. That—or she didn't have a runaway appetite. Either way, it was good.

Aside from my inviting Carla to the party I decided to throw in a few days, I must admit we gossiped for most of the drive—mainly about our beloved neighbors. Tom and Irene Clancy were having marital trouble ever since Irene hired their new maid. Irene suspected the two were having a steamy love affair.

"Is that what she told you?" I asked.

"Yes!" Carla said. "Irene blurted out the whole thing to me the other day. I was outside watering the plants when she came over. She looked a little down, so I asked her what was wrong. Well, I guess she needed someone to talk to."

"I hope it's not true. Would be a shame to break up a happy home."

"Happy home? Those two put on a show for years, Lucille. I live right next door to them, so I heard the occasional fights. Yet, every time they left that house together, they had a cheerful look on their faces! Don't know who they thought they were foolin'. Then that spoiled son of theirs, Clyde, keeps sneakin' young girls in the house when his parents are off to work."

"Did you tell Irene about these girls parading through her house?"

"'Course not! And spill the beans that I knew everything wasn't the way they portrayed it to be? I may be a single mother, but Brittany and I don't have to pretend to be contented. We just are."

"Well, how come Irene hasn't said good riddance to the maid?" I asked. "She likes the headache or is she hoping to catch them in the act, so she'd have grounds for divorce?"

"Tom's against letting her go—the maid, that is. He's adamant that the whole *affair* thing is in Irene's head. Personally, I don't know if it is."

After dropping Brittany off to practice, Carla offered to wait around while Nilla and I did our shopping instead of us catching a cab back home. Brittany's father was expected to pick her up at noon.

"Good morning, young ladies!" went a deep male's voice the second we entered Sal's Convenience Store.

"Morning, Sheriff," Carla and I replied in unison.

He stooped down to pat Nilla's head. In response, she lunged forward for his hand and he jerked back just in time.

Gerald Cooke had been Sheriff in the county for the past four years and was doing a darn good job at it. Chadsworth boasted a very low crime rate, compared to other neighboring parts. Usually petty thefts kept a few officers busy, but homicides and other serious crimes were pretty much non-existent. Chadsworth hadn't seen a single murder for at least six years, and I believe before that, there wasn't any reported homicides for around ten.

"For Heaven's sake, Nilla!" I lowered my head in her direction. "Must you always react that way every time the good Sheriff here tries to be friendly?" My diplomatic scolding of her instantly changed her growl to a whimper as she turned away.

"Hee…" The Sheriff grinned, standing up again. "I'll keep trying 'til I've won her over. One day, she'll give me the time of day."

Carla chuckled.

"Getting that early shopping done?" he asked.

"Yes, sir," I said. "I'm picking up a few things for a little party I'm having at the house Saturday night. You're more than welcomed to come by."

"Oh, I'd love to, Lucille, but I'll be on duty."

"You are the Sheriff right?" I tilted my sunglasses, out of habit.

He seemed quite taken aback by the question. "Yeah."

"Thought so. Which means you can do whatever the hell you wanna do."

"I'm afraid it doesn't work that way."

Carla stood there awkwardly. I believe it was my challenging that nice Sheriff there that made her feel a bit uncomfortable.

"What's hard about passing by for a few minutes, picking up some food and something nice to wash it down with?" I pressed.

Cooke appeared to be thinking, then with a slightly yellow show of teeth, soon replied, "I'm sure I can do that, Lucille. Thanks for the invitation." He tipped his hat. "I have to be going now. You ladies have a good day."

"Sad to say, you practically ran the Sheriff off!" Carla exclaimed as we headed toward the nearest aisle.

"I did no such thing! If he was uncomfortable, it's because of the silly response he gave to my invitation! He really insulted my intelligence. Everyone knows the Sheriff can go wherever he wants, whether he's on or off duty. What Sheriff doesn't? Furthermore, who's monitoring his every move?"

"You mean, other than a house full of party-goers?" Carla just put it out there.

She probably had a point.

We finished up around ten o'clock, then headed home.

5

I sat with David for a while in the TV room that night, while he waited for Juliet—I mean—*Sabrina* to show up. By his account, she was running late. He'd settled in quite nicely at my place and in a way, I was glad to have him there. Of course, I didn't let him know that. My plan wasn't to keep him, but to send him back to Merlene who felt she was pretty much fending for herself in that three bedroom house. If I didn't hear her gripe about David's sudden departure a million times a day, I didn't hear it once.

Sensing Anthony in the doorway, instinctively, I turned. He seemed a tad surprised when I did so since he was sure the blind lady shouldn't have been the one to look in his direction.

"I'm making some coffee…" he pointed behind with his thumb, "…and thought I'd ask if anyone wanted any."

"How nice of you, Anthony! I'd love a cup," I told him.

"Thanks, but I'll pass," David replied, politely.

Anthony returned minutes later. He was cautious in handing the coffee to me, but didn't know I could see those smooth hands of his just fine. "Could you sit with us for a minute?" I asked as he was about to leave.

I immediately knew the request didn't sound very good to David since Sabrina was sure to pop up at any moment and they'd want their privacy.

Anthony hesitated.

"Just for a moment," I said. "I'd like to share something with you both. I got to tell Theodore before he went to work."

Anthony sat directly across from me. My fine glass table stood between us.

"I wanted to let everyone know that I'll be hosting a party here this coming Saturday in celebration of my and Donnie's fiftieth wedding anniversary! Yes, I know he's dead and gone, but he's still my husband, the love of my life," With that utterance, I almost felt butterflies inside again after so many years. “And had he been here, we would’ve had a grand celebration. He loved parties and so do I. I want to honor our life together and his memory. And I’m sure wherever he is, he’ll be watching with a huge smile on his face.”

“Sounds awesome, Miss Lucille,” David said.

“Yes!” Anthony added, rather excitedly, to my surprise. I understood if he had reservations though—he just wasn’t the “crowd” type; more of an introvert. After all, he barely spoke a word around there unless spoken to.

“It won’t be anything big. Just a little gathering of a few neighbors and my new friends from the Pichton Pet Society. You both, along with Theodore are welcomed to be a part of the celebration, of course. After all, you *are* living in the Donnie’s house. He’d expect you to not exclude yourselves.” I couldn’t help but point out that last part as a bit of motivation for them to show up. *I know*—there I go with my mouth again. Merlene was right all along. I guess I just never learn.

The boys surprised me.

Anthony promised to pick up some decorations the next day and David offered to help tidy up for the guests before the party. I knew Theodore would assist in any way he could. I'm not one to discriminate, but that's why I preferred renting out rooms to men instead of women. Not just that the fellas were often helpful and easier on the eyes when I could, in fact, see them, as opposed to my looking at another lady, such as myself. But my Momma always used to say while I was growing up that two women cannot live in the same house. She was right! In my banking career, I put up with nothing, but drama—the curse of working with a lot of women and I wasn't about to during my twilight years. Life's just too darn short. Besides, Merlene supplied me with the balance I needed—bringing enough drama all on her own.

The party was in three days and I was thrilled to be sharing my and Donnie's anniversary with close friends, and old and new acquaintances. Jim Haygood, director of the Pichton Pet Society, Claire Fairweather, Montey Williams and several others said they'd be there. I'd met most of them at the new member introductory meeting. I was truly honored and if Donnie was here, he'd be too. I planned to make it an unforgettable night in celebration of two lives that had been knitted together for decades filled with love, happiness, and sacrifice—the latter, mostly on Donnie's part.

The doorbell rang a few minutes after Anthony had left the room. David got up as we heard a female's voice at the door. Anthony had shown her in and David met her at the entrance of the TV room.

"Good evening," she said.

I figured she was speaking to me since I hadn't immediately turned in her direction.

"Miss Lucille, I'd like for you to meet my girlfriend, Sabrina," David proudly said.

Before shifting slightly to my right, I clearly envisioned her and boy, wasn't she a gorgeous young lady?! It's no wonder David had fallen head over heels in love with her.

"Good evening, young lady. It's a pleasure to meet you." I tried to remember not to make eye contact with people, particularly when I knew I could see them.

"The pleasure's all mine, Miss Lucille." She smiled.

I got up to give them some privacy.

"No funny business, ya hear? Not under my roof. If you start to feel frisky, there's a motel just off Highway Nine."

They both chucked as I walked away.

Nilla darted from under the sofa as I approached the stairs. Her wet tongue licking my ankles was her way of expressing her profound affection for me—at least I liked to think so.

"I'm going to bed, Nilla. Wanna join me?" I asked.

She barked once in response. That fur of hers was becoming a bit tinged, but when it was sparkling clean, it was so much more beautiful. I loved to caress it every chance I got.

"You're going in the bathtub tonight!" I told her.

She barked again, then growled, which was no shock to me. She knew that word "bath" like she knew where to find her fresh food and water several times a day, and she absolutely detested the word. I picked her up and started up the stairway. That's when I heard my front door creak open.

"Going to bed already?" Merlene asked.

I stopped in my tracks and turned around. "What're you doing here this time of night?"

She shut the door behind her and approached us. "Couldn't sleep. Knew you'd be awake."

"Well, you barely caught me. I was about to go to bed before *stinky* here convinced me by her dingy fur to give her that bath she needs."

"It's after eight o'clock! Can't it wait 'til tomorrow?"

"Not if she's to sleep anywhere near me tonight," I replied. "Now's just as good a time to get her cleaned up as any."

"Okay. Since you insist on doing this now, let's take her upstairs to the bathroom; I'll wash her and you dry. How's that?"

"If you want, but I can handle it myself, as I always do."

"I know you do!" She barked.

Here we go again.

"Can't a person be helpful around here?"

I sighed. "Sure. No problem at all. You can bathe her and I'll dry." There was no point in arguing with her. She already had enough on her mind.

Then I thought of David and wondered if I should mention anything, but quickly realized it would be pointless not to. She was bound to bring up his name sooner or later. "David and *Juliet* are in the TV room," I whispered loudly.

A cold, almost menacing expression crossed her face. "I see."

She stood quietly for a few moments.

"Well, aren't you going to say 'hi'?" I shuddered to think her hatred for the young lady in there was enough for her to avoid her own son.

"Sure, I will," she said, dismally.

"Girl, you'd better swallow your pride from now on and get yourself together! Don't be a fool. You know you'd better pass the test."

"I know." She started to walk off in the direction of the TV room. I waited by the staircase.

"Hi, David," I heard her say. "Sabrina…"

The kids hailed back. The David I knew would've gotten right up and given his mom a hug. He'd always been very affectionate toward her and I knew that's what *Meddling Merlene* was missing the most.

"Uhh!" he said, apparently after he'd gently squeezed her.

"You kids are doing all right?" she asked.

I could've cried! She was making me proud.

"Yes, ma'am!" Sabrina sounded especially cheerful, probably because Merlene had bothered to ask.

Nilla tried to wiggle herself out of my arms, but I held her within my grip. "Don't worry, Snookums. We're going upstairs now."

I made my way upstairs with Nilla. Merlene knew where the bathroom was. When we almost reached the landing, footsteps echoed behind us.

"I'm right behind you!" she said.

"Figured as much," I responded.

We got Nilla into her bath and watched her try her hardest to get out of that bubbly doggie pool. This is what she hated the most—getting clean!

"So, you're not going to say how it went?" I said to Merlene as she worked the shampoo through Nilla's fur.

"It went okay, I guess," she replied, evenly.

"Okay."

She switched the topic to ask about the party arrangements, though she'd been kept up-to-date as far as that went. I filled her in anyway, though I must've sounded like a scorched record to her. The stoic expression on her face didn't conceal her pain as I knew she felt that David had simply chosen that girl over his own mother—regardless of the blabbering he gave about Merlene controlling his life. She was going to believe whatever her mind told her and that was the size of it.

"It's good that everyone here has offered to help, in some way," she said as she handed my *snookums* to me. I had Nilla's big, brown towel waiting to wrap her in. It was her favorite part of the bath.

"Yes, it's very considerate of them," I replied. Then I lowered my voice. "Maybe they're all hoping for a slight reduction in their rent. Well, they can dream on!"

We both laughed.

Nilla went running toward my hallway carpet the second she was released. She shook off the excess water from her fur before rolling over the rug.

After having a cup of hot chocolate with me, Merlene went home and Sabrina left a short time later. Now that the coast was clear, Nilla and I were finally able to get some sleep.

6

The day before the party, I sat outside on the back patio after breakfast. The front door closed shortly thereafter which meant Theodore had finally left for work. David and Anthony had been gone from an hour earlier.

I was accustomed to my front door swinging open and shut ever since I'd started taking on tenants a year or so after Donnie died. Not that I needed the money, since Donnie had left me well secured financially. The main reason was that I was afraid of being alone. I was on my own then—just Nilla and me. That was a scary feeling, not that Nilla wasn't enough company. But what if something happened to me or the house? There was only so much she could do.

None of the properties in my neighborhood were zoned for commercial purposes, so technically, I shouldn't have been able to acquire tenants. But when you've been around long enough and have forged some pretty good relationships with the "higher ups" in society, pretty much anything is possible. They did take my disability into consideration, though.

I'd let Nilla run off into the back yard while I sat there wishing I could watch her play. For the past two days, I'd seen nothing—absolutely nothing, except this blackness before me which seemed to be the only guarantee in my life.

The morning air was fresh and crisp. Getting outside and inhaling it was what kept most negative thoughts at bay. I've had better days for sure.

"Why do you do this to me?" I murmured, hoping in my heart for a supernatural answer. "Why would you allow me to see only—*sometimes*?" In the back of my mind I felt guilty for complaining since I knew my situation could've been far worse, and it was for a while. *Why couldn't the inner vision at least be constant?* I wondered. It was bad enough that my eyes were literally useless, but having a taste of sight now and again had somewhat spoiled me. I wanted to see all the time. I'd started to feel like I was being juggled around, teased, and taunted.

Nilla barked at something, then the front door slammed.

I wondered who it was.

"Merlene, is that you?" I started to get up. Those guys knew to lock the door on their way out, but maybe Theodore forgot.

"It's just me," David answered, moments later.

"What are you doing here, David?" I sat down again.

"The boss decided to call when I was on my way to say they're doing an internal audit today, so the office will be closed." He sighed heavily.

"Fine time to tell you, huh?"

"Yep. Mind if I joined you out here?" he asked.

"Not at all. Would love the company."

For a while, there was complete silence.

"What's on your mind, son?" I could feel the tension he was carrying.

I also detected his shock at the question.

"Nothing at all, Miss Lucille. What makes you ask?"

"You're going to be honest with me or not?"

Silence took center stage again. It was then my entire backyard gradually came into view — the plants, the trees, the flowers, bees and butterflies hovering over them and Nilla in the corner by the fence digging into the dirt.

She soon ran over to me and started licking my toes. I usually wore sandals because I knew she liked those toes of mine. Glad she didn't think of biting like she did whenever she spotted Theodore's. I wondered why she always targeted him and no one else in the house. I figured it must be his scent. Either Theodore's was sweeter than the rest of ours or vice-versa. There were some things about Nilla I just never understood.

"Okay," he said. "But I'd hate to burden you with my problems."

"At my age, son, I'm used to carrying burdens. I won't crack and fall to pieces; I promise."

I sensed the boy's reluctance. "She's cheating on me, Miss Lucille! I just know it!"

I leaned in a little, thinking I hadn't heard right. "What? Who? You mean, Juliet?"

"*Juliet?* Her name's Sabrina," he quickly corrected me.

Actually, the name was a slip of the tongue on my part.

"How can you be sure? She seemed like a nice young lady."

"I don't know." He shifted in his chair. "She's been acting *different* lately. We don't go out on dates anymore like we used to. She always wants to stay indoors—either at my place or hers. It's like she doesn't wanna be seen in public with me. It's usually the girl complaining about the guy not taking her out as much as he should, so this is all really weird to me."

"You could be wrong, David. Maybe the poor girl's tired after working all day and would just rather spend quiet time with you curled up, watching TV," I suggested. "To think she's cheating just because she'd rather stay home most nights instead of going out is taking the whole thing too far into left field, in my opinion."

There I was feeling sorry for myself before David got home, but hearing his concern made me forget my own problems temporarily. I remember that crushing feeling when I thought the man I was in love with before I met Donnie was cheating on me. It's all I thought about all day, every day until he finally came right out and told me he and I were over; then six months later, he married someone else. It literally took a couple of years for me to get over that heartbreak. I truly hoped Juliet was as sweet as pie and David's insecurity was unjustified.

"I guess you're right," he finally said, after some thought. "Maybe I'm just letting my imagination run away with me."

"I'd say you are."

Maybe it took hearing from an old lady that he might've been a bit paranoid made him feel better.

Nilla had gone off somewhere in the enclosed yard. She loved playtime outdoors, though for the most part, she was a house dog—I guess, one of those *sheltered* ones, like some of the kids I described around my neighborhood to the rather eager listeners at the Pichton Pet Society. I felt good about that group, in spite of Merlene's negative assertions. She might've been right about the *uppity* side of them, but they couldn't have been too bad because they loved and cared for animals.

"Can I ask you a question, Miss Lucille?" David said.

"Sure, David! What is it?"

"Remember a few years ago you told me you can see things sometimes, but not with your eyes, and you asked me not to broadcast it?"

"Yeah… Have you?"

"Have I what?"

"Broadcasted it?" I asked.

"No." He grinned. "I kept my word and Mom made sure to ingrain into my brain how important it was to do so. I just never understood what you told me though and Mom couldn't really explain it either. She said you have visions sometimes; she called it 'inner visions'."

"Uh huh."

"I guess my question is...how did these inner visions start? And how do you know if you're actually seeing things in reality when it happens?"

That was a trick question; probably more of a *test*. Thankfully, it was asked at the perfect time. I kept my focus straight ahead toward the backyard and asked: "Are you wearing a dark blue shirt with a collar and a light beige pants?" David never wore a uniform at work. "And on the inside tag of your shirt, does it read *Marcus Cole Design*?"

I saw the look on his face.

"My God! You've nailed it—even down to the brand name. My shirt's a Marcus Cole. I'm stunned!"

"Now, do you understand my inner vision?" I asked.

He quickly nodded. "Yes! Yes, I do, but wouldn't you call that being psychic?"

"No, you wouldn't," I replied. "Well, at least, you shouldn't. I don't know people's past, neither their future. I barely know what's happening in the present! I can't even rely on this inner sight because sometimes I can go for days without seeing a darn thing. That's what makes me so frustrated sometimes. I feel like I'm being teased, you know?"

He nodded. Since he was there, I figured I might as well off-load on him a little bit. After all, I pretty much calmed his fears about the lovely *Juliet* a short while ago.

"But how did it happen?"

He was good to remind me of the second part of his question.

"The night of Donnie's heart attack. Up to that time, I'd been completely, utterly, terrifyingly blind for two full years. I depended on Donnie to do practically everything for me. But I never even thought about what would happen if there came a time when he really needed me for a change—if something were to happen where he couldn't help himself and I was the only one around." I paused. "That's what happened that night."

I had David's full attention.

"I was never a light sleeper, so when he sat up suddenly in the middle of the night, naturally, I woke up." Many times I wished I could forget that day, but I never could. The events etched in time will remain with me until I've taken my final breath. "I asked if he was all right, but he didn't respond. Instead, I heard what sounded like gurgling sounds coming from his throat and I knew something was wrong. I sat up quickly, feeling for the man who was always so strong, but then I heard that sound more and more and when I touched him, he was crouched over the bed. I was starting to panic because no matter how many times I asked him what was wrong, he wouldn't answer; he *couldn't* answer. I had to do something. That's when all of a sudden, in my mind's eye, I saw those people for the very first time…"

"People?"

"Uh huh. About twelve of them were in the room just standing along the wall adjacent to our closet. I recognized one of them from news footage long before I'd lost my sight."

"Who was it?" David probed.

"It was Sir Clement Tucker. No mistake about it. I don't know if you've heard of him, but he was a prominent member of this community."

"Yes, I heard he was a wealthy immigrant who owned a lot of property in these parts."

"Including the one we're sitting on," I indicated.

"But he's…dead."

"Yeah, I know. Well, I don't know why he was here and to this day, I have no idea who the others were. But I realized they were all I could see as my Donnie was struggling to breathe. I asked them, whomever they were to help me, but the whole time I pleaded, they just stood there, staring at me. I knew they had to have been ghosts, but I was desperate. I felt for the phone on my nightstand, but couldn't think clearly enough to locate the digits. I was crying, horrified that Donnie needed me and I couldn't help him. Then suddenly, images inside the bedroom came into view. First, they were like silhouettes, then I realized I could see everything, including my Donnie. I saw the digits on the phone and quickly dialed 911 and finally, help was on the way. Donnie survived for a few hours after that, then he passed away."

David leaned in and placed his arm around my shoulder. "I'm sorry, Miss Lucille. I can only imagine how difficult that was for you losing him."

"It was very hard for me," I replied. "When he died, I immediately sank into a deep depression. I stopped eating, wasn't sleeping; I just wanted my life to be over too. I wanted to be with Donnie. But it was your mother who was here for me every day, rowing me and trying her best to force me to eat something."

I couldn't help, but grin a little, while sharing that with David. It was amazing how Merlene's rowing and scolding actually became therapeutic for me at that time in my life. "I truly owe a lot to your mother," I continued. "She became my Donnie; except that she forced me to become independent for the first time since I lost my vision. Donnie had made everything easy for me, whereas Merlene threw me out on a limb, if you know what I mean…"

"I do," he said. "Sounds like Mom. She hadn't shared all of that with me though. I never knew this."

"Your mother—my archenemy—is really something special. Has a heart of gold." I thought he needed to hear that, and it did come from my heart.

"Hello, Miss Pfiffer!" Judy Anderson hailed from the balcony of her parents' home. She was a friendly pre-teen brunette who wore those braces of hers well. When she got them put in a year earlier, she ran over to my house to describe how awesome they were—that is, after the initial pain from the installation had subsided.

“Hello, dear! How’re you doing?” I waved.

“I’m fine, thanks”

She was standing near the rail. Debbie Anderson joined her out there and hailed as well. Our homes sat about thirty feet away from the boundary line on the eastern and western sides. I had much more yard space in the back even though our properties were the exact, same size. The Andersons had taken up less space in the front yard where Donnie and I had done the opposite. I was glad we made that decision as the backyard was Nilla’s sanctuary. She had more than enough room to get lost in.

“Hi, Vanilla!” Judy was waving.

Nilla looked up for a good second, then darted further to the right and started inspecting something behind the Fothergilla bushes.

I felt my inner vision fading again. No! It usually lasted much longer once it came. I tried to hold onto it just by mere will, but knew I couldn’t.

“Don’t forget the party’s tomorrow night,” I told Debbie. “Make sure to drag that husband of yours out too. Let him know I’ll have some rabbit food available to compliment the diet he's been working so hard at."

Debbie chuckled. "I will. We'll all be there."

Debbie and Judy gave a kind farewell and returned inside the house, pulling the sliding door shut.

David must've been in deep contemplation of our previous conversation when he said, "Miss Lucille...do you think the people you saw that night helped you out?"

"I think so." I replied. "I believe if they hadn't shown up, my inner vision wouldn't have been triggered and I wouldn't have been able to make the call in time for Donnie. Because of them, I was able to spend a few more hours with him. I thanked him for everything he'd done for me and told him I loved him. I knew the prognosis. The doctors had made it clear that it was highly probable he wouldn't survive. But yeah, definitely, those people helped me."

"How often have you seen them since?"

I hesitated for a moment, then said, "I see them occasionally. And even if I can't see anything else, I see them. Sometimes, others show up too."

"Where do you see them mostly?"

"In my bedroom and at times, around the neighborhood when I take Nilla for her walks. They're somehow tied to this area. I know Sir Clement's connection to it, but have no idea about the others. One day, I'll get to the bottom of it. And *no*… just in case you're wondering… I'm not afraid to see them. At first I was for a while, but I realize they're just like you and me, only not in their physical bodies anymore."

"You're a brave woman, Miss Lucille." David sighed. "I doubt I'd be able to face what you've had to—any of it."

"You would if you had to, son. Believe me. You do what you have to do. I had to put on my big girl's panty and anyone else in my situation would have to pull up the right underwear."

Later on, David went out and bought us some lunch. We had a wonderful time together that day until he'd had enough of me and took off for a while. Undoubtedly, Merlene had raised him well and I was certain he'd be on his way back home soon.

7

My house must have been the talk of the neighborhood that evening. Anthony, David and Theodore had done a splendid job putting up decorations inside and out, on the balcony, through the trees, shrubs—everywhere! The over-the-top decorating was strictly Anthony's idea. The man had class and it showed.

Inside the house was even more breath-taking. A Happy 50th Anniversary banner hung from one column in the living room to the other and Donnie's hand-painted portrait hung slightly above it. That room, by far, was the largest in the house and other than the back porch, was one of my favorites to escape to. Fresh vases of flowers had been placed in various spots throughout the front area of the house; colorful balloons attached to the walls were hanging in clusters and then some individually throughout the house. The place was immaculate. The boys and Merlene had made sure of it.

Dressed in a lovely, sleeveless, burgundy dress which fell slightly below the knees, Merlene walked in with the triple-layered cake from Osmond's Creations. Pineapple cream cheese filling—it was Donnie's absolute favorite, and every year, we were sure to pick one up for his birthday.

Theodore brought in the plastic bag from Merlene's car which hid a couple of extra packs of decorative paper plates and cups, just in case our supply in the kitchen ran low. I knew he wouldn't have gotten Merlene to give up that cake. She would've definitely been the one to bring it out of the car herself to avoid the mere possibility of it getting mashed in any way.

The caterers I'd hired were ready to serve as the guests were beginning to show up and gather in the living room. Just about everyone complimented me on how beautiful the place looked, but I knew I didn't deserve the credit and said so. Without my friends, none of it would've been possible. I was beyond gratified and Donnie must've been so proud. We were about to celebrate our wedding anniversary in grand style.

I insisted on being at the door when the bulk of guests arrived, so David went and brought out one of my dining room chairs and set it down inside a few feet away from the door. Nilla took a comfy spot on the fluffy mat right next to me.

That night, and even leading up to it, I literally felt like I had children and it was a good feeling. I never felt my life had been *incomplete* without having any of my own because I always had my Donnie. And in a way, I didn't think I could be a fit mother anyway since Jennifer Meadows was not a really good mom to me. But it felt great being looked after like that and catered to by these fine young men who were spending a little part of their life with me—for however long that was.

"Oh! How lovely!" Debbie Anderson remarked as she walked in. Her daughter, Judy, and largely absent husband, Gary, were with her. Judy immediately went to Nilla and started to play with her. The two wandered off somewhere while Debbie and Gary chatted with me.

"Thanks, my dear." I smiled. "I can imagine how lovely it really is." I hated when people stared at me, thinking I couldn't see, when in fact, sometimes I could. Although I knew they weren't aware that I could see them, I felt guilty nonetheless. But I was ready for the government. If they suspected I'd been lying about my blindness, all they had to do was send me to a specialist who would confirm, in no uncertain terms, just as Dr. Junca did that for me to see, it would be a miracle. At my age, I was no longer willing to fight battles that weren't worth fighting, but this one surely would be.

"Happy Anniversary, Lucille," Gary Anderson said.

"Gary, is that you?" I reached out for his hand and he took mine.

"Yep. It's me."

He was such a handsome guy when he smiled. Other than that, he wasn't much of a looker and quite frankly, I was never too sure of what Debbie saw in him. He was a fabulous provider though; most men in our neighborhood were, except for Big Nose Frankie who had his common-law wife Drita for his sugar momma. Nobody liked Frankie and he didn't like any of us just the same. Minded his own business, for the most part, which suited everyone just fine. I remember Donnie having a run-in with him once when he was driving by and caught the big brute kicking their German Shepherd. What the hell did that sweet dog ever do to him? Donnie stopped the car and hollered at him and all Frankie did was give him the middle finger. Donnie had told me all about it after he got home from the store. He said he threatened to call Animal Welfare to take the dog from Frankie, but felt more like getting out of that car and confronting the middle-aged giant man to man. I was glad when Donnie did call Animal Welfare and they went in a couple of hours later and collected the dog. By all accounts, the animal was on the verge of starvation anyway, so the timing was almost perfect for getting it out of there and to the shelter where the treatment would've been far better.

That was my Donnie. He cared about everything and everyone; that's why I had to make this day extra special for him.

"Well, it's good you came up for fresh air," I told Gary, who seemed puzzled by the remark. I did notice the smirk on Debbie's face as she tried to conceal it.

"You're still dieting?" I asked him.

"Actually, I am. Going on two weeks now. I've lost a few pounds," he proudly informed me.

"That's marvelous! I've got the perfect selection of food for you here. I didn't want to ruin your diet."

"That's really nice of you, Lucille."

"It's nothing. Least I can do for a neighbor."

Debbie was checking her watch.

"What is it, honey?" Gary appeared concerned, probably because Debbie, at that moment, did.

"I hope Angela remembers to lock the top latch when she leaves," she said. "No neighborhood is completely safe, you know."

"That's why you should've left the key somewhere for her like I suggested. We could've always gotten it back in the morning. We have a set. And besides, we're gonna eventually have to get her a key of her own anyway. "

"Who's Angela?" I asked.

"She's our new housekeeper," Gary said. "She called before we came here to say she'd left her purse in the laundry room. So, she's on her way back to get it. We left the front door unlocked, but I think it would've made more sense to hide the key under the doormat for her."

"I see," I replied.

"Lucille, Gary can't seem to understand that I'm not leaving our house keys to a total stranger!" Debbie said. "We don't even know if she's going to work out as the new housekeeper.

It's best, in my opinion, to give it a few weeks before we turn over our keys to any new help. Besides, I'm there all the time anyway. What does she need the house key for?"

"So, I guess you won't be leaving the house for even a minute, Deb," I said. "You won't be running any errands, taking Judy to school, etc. as long as your new housekeeper is in your house?"

"'Course I will!" She frowned.

"Well, you'll just go out and leave her without the keys? What if she goes out to dump the trash and mistakenly locks herself out of the house? I remember one time this lady left a housekeeper home alone with her infant son and the housekeeper went outside to do something or the other and found she couldn't get back into the house. If she had the keys in her apron, she could've let herself back in. But instead, in a panic, she had to go to a neighbor, who thankfully, was at home at the time, use their phone and call her boss at work. Look, my point is…if you trusted the woman enough to hire her to be in your home for whatever number of hours a day, I'd think you can trust her enough to not take off with all your material possessions when you're not there to watch her."

"Well put!" Gary agreed.

Debbie seemed to have come to her senses, though I could completely understand her reluctance to trust a stranger with her keys. However, I know from having renters in my own house that trust has to start somewhere.

Finally, they were off with David as he led them to the living room. Honestly, that family had taken up enough of my time at the door. I certainly wasn't there as a domestic counselor.

Nilla strolled back over and took her seat again next to me. She was better behaved that night than usual. Perhaps it was because she recalled the last time we had any type of gathering, was right after Donnie's funeral for the repast.

I guess the crew from the Pichton Pet Society had arranged to meet at my house at a certain time, since they arrived one after the other. Claire Fairweather entered first with a rather handsome older man on her arm.

"Lucille! Happy Anniversary to you and your dear husband!" She leaned in and lightly pressed her cheek against mine.

"Thank you." I smiled.

"This is my wonderful husband, Frederick."

"Freddie, for short," he indicated.

Anthony, dressed in a long sleeved, black dress shirt and black trousers, led all the guests to the main sitting area where they were free to pour their preferred drinks. Theodore had stocked up nicely, being a man who knew his wines and spirits quite well. There was no heavy alcohol; I only allowed milder beverages due to the occasion.

Montey Williams showed up next with a stunning, young African-American woman on his arm. He introduced her as his fiancé. Montey was in his thirties and she looked to be in her mid to late twenties. Seemed like a lovely couple.

Jim Haygood, director of the Pichton Pet Society walked in a few minutes later with his wife, Edna. She looked like the epitome of *class* and literally turned heads when she entered the house. It could be because she might've gone overboard with that long, sparkling ball gown she had on. I waited with Merlene until Edna had disappeared into the living room before laughing myself to tears.

"She thinks she's something, isn't she?" Merlene remarked.

I tried to catch my breath before chiming in. "That nose of hers couldn't get any higher up in the air. She looks like a damn peacock!"

We were both in tears by then. I knew it was wrong to laugh at a guest, especially one who'd gone through all the trouble of trying *to steal the show*, which I might add, she'd done rather successfully, but I just couldn't help myself. I'm sure if Jim Haygood imagined for a second I was having such a time at his wife's expense, he would've kicked me out of that high society club for sure.

David stood nearby to assist Anthony with seating and anything else he needed, while Theodore was outside ensuring that people were able to park in a good spot. I didn't let on, but David looked bothered by something. I could tell he was trying not to make it obvious. I also noticed him on that cell phone every so often, but what young person isn't? But in this case, he seemed a little more obsessive with it, considering we were having a party that night. I figured it had something to do with Juliet, but I couldn't be sure.

Four other members of the Pichton Pet Society soon arrived: Marsha Simms, secretary;

John Ashwood, a local veterinarian; Sammy Furrow, Assistant Chairperson to Claire Fairweather and Ronald Lancaster, regular member like me. I humbly received their warm anniversary greetings.

Carla and Brittany Walkes, and Robert and Diane Clover—my good neighbors, showed up next. The Clovers had brought along their two sons, Brady and Drake, both home from college for the summer. They'd grown up like twins, though they were a mere eighteen months apart. The younger one, Brady—a mere genius, had skipped a grade in high school and ended up in the same stream as his older brother. Luckily for Diane and Rob, they'd both graduated together and got shipped off to college at the same time. Diane loved her boys, but she looked so relieved to get rid of the rascals for several months at a time.

By a quarter to nine, at least fifty people were in my house, and there was plenty of room for more. At first, when Donnie had our house constructed, I had no idea what just the two of us would do with all that living space, but Donnie insisted it would come in handy for parties and the like, and he was right. We had so many of them over the years. They all stopped when I'd lost my eyesight.

"Are you ready, Mrs. Pfiffer?" Anthony asked.

A little overwhelmed, I nodded, slid my arm under his and we walked into the living room. Everyone was standing when we entered; Theodore had obviously made sure of that, since David looked more and more like his *nerves were on him*. There was another portrait of my beloved on the wall at the back of the room. That one was my favorite. He was posing with a hand under his chin. That Asian artist was famous for her realistic paintings and she'd done a fine job of rendering Donnie's likeness.

Applause erupted and they all sang the happy anniversary song—mainly a chorus, similar to the happy birthday song. I felt like a queen as I sat in my favorite chair that Anthony had draped over with my expensive dark-brown marble fabric. All I needed now was a crown — *just kidding!* — and everything would be perfect.

Merlene took center stage when she gave a speech about meeting Donnie and me for the first time, and she got a lot of jokes in there as well.

It was when I was almost done telling everyone how Donnie and I had met and how that smile of his had captivated my heart that *Juliet* quietly walked into the room. I thought David's nerves were on him, but it was obvious this girl had some intense stuff on her mind as well. The excessive make-up on her face couldn't conceal it.

Who shows up at a party looking aggravated? I mean, *really.* Was she serious? Was she trying to get all of us in a bad mood?

8

She stood near the archway, and David was at the back of the room. They made eye contact. Most heads had turned her way when she walked in, but I snagged the guests' attention with the continuation of the Donnie and Lucille love story.

"I want to thank you all from the bottom of my heart for coming here tonight and for choosing to celebrate this wonderful occasion with Donnie and me. My house is yours—feel free to stroll wherever you please, apart from our bedrooms, of course. A tent, I'm told has been erected in the front yard, and seating is in place, if you prefer the cool night's breeze. Our lovely caterers will take care of those growling stomachs I've been hearing all night."

Laughter erupted and moments later, soft music oozed from the ceiling speakers. Theodore had gone above and beyond to set that up nicely in spite of the short time-frame we all had to work with.

David finally made his way over to his girlfriend and they spoke softly. As I sat there enjoying the music, I saw Theodore walk up to David.

"The tent's fallen," he said. "Give me a hand, will ya?"

David excused himself and went with Theodore, leaving Juliet to mingle—something I could tell she had no interest in doing. She stood with arms folded next to the miniature waterfall situated a few feet away from where the long table of hors d'oeuvres and other goodies sat. It must've been a minute or two after David had left that Brady Clover, approached her and said something she obviously didn't appreciate. I figured he must've made a pass or something. Moments later, he yelled out loud: "Stuck up, bi*&%#!"

Juliet swiftly raised her right hand and slapped him in the face. She even made *mister arrogant* stagger a bit, and I could tell he was startled, but more than anything, embarrassed.

All eyes were now on them.

He was about to retaliate when his brother, Drake, caught his hand in mid-air.

"She's not worth it, li'l bro," he said. "Let's just go outside."

"She slapped me though!" Brady replied with every bit of virulence he had inside.

"She's a dumb broad. Just leave it alone."

"Dumb broad, huh?" Juliet fired back. "I'll show you who's a dumb broad!" She was ready to give the other brother a taste of what Brady got.

Claire Fairweather and her husband advanced from near the piano. I could've sworn the woman had an actual smirk on her face as the action unfolded. Her husband, stood a few feet behind; he didn't seem to want any part of it.

Diane and Robert Clover, the boys' parents, were nowhere in sight, but Drake, managed to subdue the situation. He placed his arm around Brady's shoulders. "Let's go before she starts growing horns."

They laughed as they headed into the hallway.

Anthony hurried in just as the boys were leaving. "Is everything all right?" he asked Juliet, who appeared justified by her actions.

"I'm super," she replied, then went to pour herself a drink.

The crowd went on about their business and Merlene, who'd been in the kitchen with the caterers for a few minutes came and walked with me over to the dining room table where several guests were already seated. Claire and Frederick Fairweather and Pichton's director, Jim Haygood and his wife, Edna, joined us.

"It's a good thing you couldn't see that woman making a spectacle of herself a short time ago, Lucille!" Claire grinned, much to Merlene's dismay.

I could tell my friend couldn't believe the dicty woman actually referenced someone's blindness as if it was a good thing. Sitting to Merlene's immediate left, I quickly patted her knee. It was a sign that she should continue holding her tongue. Thankfully, she'd taken the cue.

A few at the table joked about the incident and said the boys should've been thrown out, especially Brady. But others who'd been in close proximity to the three, alleged that Juliet had blown the matter out of proportion and she didn't need to cause a scene.

"If a guy had insulted me just because I rejected his advances, I might've slapped him too," one woman said.

"What would give you the right to slap him?" Claire asked. "Sure, you might not like what he said, but putting your hands on another person outside of self-defense is a criminal act, as far as I know."

The majority agreed with her.

A short time later, I excused myself from the table and headed upstairs to use the bathroom. After stepping onto the landing, I heard muffled sounds coming from David's room and went to see what was going on.

"You're nothing but a whore!" David snapped at Juliet, who was standing there facing him. Guess on that rather harsh note, I'd better stop referring to her as *Juliet* and call her by her given name. They certainly weren't acting like Romeo and Juliet anymore.

I immediately hid behind the wall, near the doorway.

"You think I can't see you don't wanna be here—with me *in public*? What the hell did you come for?"

"Because you kept hounding me about it; that's why!" she retorted. "After you texted me about a thousand times, I just had to show up! I told you I had a headache and you kept bugging me! You didn't even care!"

"Headache, huh?"

"Yeah! And I can't understand why you keep talking that nonsense about me not wanting to be with you in public. You're paranoid! That's what you are!"

David sighed. "Because you didn't wanna be here, you decided to cause a big problem. Everyone's talking about it."

"Oh really? A jerk says something inappropriate to me and I'm supposed to say nothing?"

"You didn't have to attack the guy. Men make advances toward women all the time. If you didn't like what he said, you could've walked away or come find me. I'm the man; let me handle it! But you didn't do that because you wanted to embarrass me. And you wanted a reason to leave," he deduced. "Well, I'm not holding you back. Do what you want."

I quickly moved along, watching my inner vision fade until I was in utter darkness again. Just as I arrived at the bathroom door, I heard footsteps hurriedly descending the staircase.

9

With a smaller number of people, mainly the younger ones outside in the front yard under the tent, the majority of my guests who'd already eaten, including those from the Pet Society, had joined me and Merlene in the living room where they played Backgammon and a few rounds of Strip Poker (okay, I'm kidding about the Strip Poker), when Nilla's excessive barking somewhere near the sliding door area caught our attention.

I'd just been sitting there wishing I could beat Merlene publicly at Backgammon since she was always such a competitor and a sore loser. She reminded me of little Johnny Eden from elementary school who cried everytime he lost a race. Guess it wasn't my day to show her up.

"What on earth is going on with Nilla barking like that? Nilla!" I cried. "Come to Momma!"

But the barking continued.

"I'll go and find out what she's up to." Merlene got up from the sofa and headed out back. I'd told Anthony to keep the sliding door open for Nilla to be able to have her fun in the backyard if she so pleased. Thought it was the only fair thing to do since everyone else was having a good, old time. That's when I heard the ear-piercing scream and everyone took off in the direction of the horrific sound. Using my cane, I made it out where I heard all the commotion going on.

"What is it?" I asked.

Then there were screams overriding other exclamations of shock and bewilderment.

"Get the dog away from there!" Carla yelled.

"What the hell's going on?" I insisted, by this time both confused and annoyed that no one seemed to remember that I didn't have the same use of my eyes as they did theirs.

"Lucille!" Merlene, grabbed me by the arm as gently as she could.

Then I heard footsteps running toward us from inside the house. I figured it must've been the other guests who'd gathered out front. "Oh, my God!" David cried. "Oh, no!"

"Merlene, if you don't tell me what's happened, I'll plant my cane up your…"

"Lucille!" she exclaimed. "Sabrina's…"

"Sabrina's what?"

"She's dead! Looks like she'd fallen from the balcony!"

My ears went numb. All of a sudden, I felt both blind and deaf. She couldn't have just said what I thought she said.

"What?" I felt my knees collapsing under me.

"I've got you!" Theodore caught me, just before my decades old derriere met the ground. He stood there with a strong arm around my waist.

"Where's Nilla? Bring her to me right this second!"

"Here she is," Judy said.

I grabbed Nilla in desperation and held her as securely as I could. I still couldn't fathom what I'd heard about Sabrina could be true. Could it really be that someone was lying dead in my back yard? My stomach started to feel queasy. This was not the time for a bathroom break. Darn it!

"How could this have happened?" Merlene cried, as if she actually felt badly for the poor girl. And I do believe she did.

David was crying uncontrollably and it wasn't long before Merlene left me and was over there at her son's side trying to console him.

The voices around me became muffled as I saw *them* again – the same ones I saw the night my sweet Donnie was having a heart attack. And finally, I could see Sabrina, lying there motionless in a crooked pose. They were standing around her in a circle, looking down. Sir Clement, as dapper as ever, stood on the western side, facing me. He was the only one not gazing down at poor, dead Sabrina. Instead, he was looking at me. I never understood why these special souls appeared to me. Though I felt I knew why Sir Clement might still have a connection to Harriet's Cove, since he was the actual developer of the subdivision, I had no idea who the others were and why they chose to use my place as the occasional hang out.

When my head became unusually light and my legs finally gave out, the last words I remembered hearing were, "Catch her!"

10

After I'd regained consciousness and had run off the EMTs, Sheriff Cooke and two strange men wearing dark suits entered my bedroom. They must have passed Merlene on the way up who'd returned downstairs to be with her son. Right away, I asked Anthony to reach for my sunglasses. He'd alerted me that the Sheriff had arrived and police officers were pretty much all over the property. No one had been allowed to leave, but were directed to assemble in the living room while the coroners took care of the deceased.

"Lucille..." Cooke started.

"Sheriff, I'm sorry it took a death to have you show up at my party." The words sort of rolled off my tongue... probably haphazardly.

I could tell from the look on Anthony's face that it was probably in poor taste.

"I'm sorry about that," I quickly sought to do damage control.

"It's okay, Lucille," Cooke replied. "Are you all right? Heard you had a fainting spell."

"I'm all right, Sheriff. It must've been the mere shock of it all that got me for a minute there." The two men that accompanied him looked eager to get down to business. "Are you alone?"

"No. I'm here with Detectives Lance Matthews and Tyrone Stewart. We're trying to get to the bottom of what happened to your guest, Sabrina Abrams."

"Mrs. Pfiffer..." Lance stepped forward. "What we'd like to do is get a group interrogation going, so we can get everything on the table one time and find out if anyone knows anything. Are you feeling well enough to join us downstairs?"

While his partner was sort of "average" as far as looks were concerned, Lance was an African-American with the shiniest, short, curly hair I've seen, high cheek bones and clean-shaven. Looked like a real heart-breaker. I nodded sort of slowly, kind of understanding his undisclosed reasoning behind wanting to do a group interrogation. It was pure laziness, in my book! But I couldn't really blame the officers.

Who'd want to individually question forty or fifty people when they could ask each question a total of one or two times the most? Smart, lazy guys they were, as far as I was concerned.

"I can go downstairs. No problem," I replied.

"Are you sure, Lucille?" Cooke asked.

"I'm positive."

Yeah, I was *positive* they were a bunch of loafers on the people's tax paying pockets!

"But before we do that," Lance came again, "Is there anything you know or heard of pertaining to what might've happened to Sabrina?"

"She's blind," Anthony interjected. "She can't possibly know anything of the sort."

There was little, quiet Anthony speaking up for me—a man who apparently only came out of his shell when arranging a party—obviously something he had a true passion for.

"Let the lady answer! She has a tongue, doesn't she?" the other detective said, rather gruffly.

I turned in that officer's direction without looking him squarely in his face. "Officer, I appreciate your wanting to get to the bottom of this most tragic matter, but I will have you know that you will *not* come into my house and address Anthony in that way. Do you understand?"

I watched him cut his eye, without the guts to respond.

Sheriff Cooke cleared his throat. "Lucille, by any chance, did you happen to have heard anything suspicious—anything at all?"

"Sheriff, I asked your detective a question, to which I've not received an answer. If any of you plan on getting any response out of me regarding anything, that gentleman or should I say *supposed* gentleman knows what to do."

Cooke gestured with his eyes and a tilt of his head to the detective to just go ahead and appease the old lady, which the man seemed not to believe the Sheriff had actually expected him to do. Guess he was used to speaking to citizens in any manner and getting away with it, but not in my house!

"I understand," he finally said.

"That's better," I replied. "And the answer is *no*—I don't know anything; neither have I heard anything suspicious. We all were having a grand time celebrating my and my husband's fiftieth wedding anniversary. We danced, chatted, played games and over-ate. That's about the size of it."

"Thanks, Lucille," Cooke said. Guess he was in a hurry to shut me up more than anything else, especially now that I'd admitted knowing absolutely nothing about anything. "Can we go downstairs now?"

"Absolutely!" I started to get up.

In spite of my resistance, Anthony helped me down the staircase and into the living room. Before we even got there, I could hear the sobbing and whispering.

Thankfully, there were enough chairs to seat everyone, including a few crashers, if they happened to stop by. The spacious room had been set up like a hall with chairs neatly arranged in rows and space on one side for the caterers' table, along with adequate walking room. I could see Sabrina over there right now near the waterfall, after she'd finally shown up, looking like she'd rather be anywhere else in the world, but there.

Merlene was seated up front with David who was a complete wreck. The boy's face was soaked in tears; he couldn't stop crying and my heart went out to him. I could tell he loved the girl, in spite of everything. Claire and the others from the Pet Society were among the crowd, as well as the Andersons, and Diane and Robert

Clover. No one had left the party… except for the Clover boys. They were nowhere to be seen.

"Where are Brady and Drake Clover?" I asked Anthony after we'd taken our seats and Cooke and the detectives were off in a corner having a quiet, little preliminary discussion.

"Don't know. I think they might've left after the incident with David's girlfriend," he said.

"I guess it doesn't matter, especially since it's obvious that the sweet girl's death was nothing more than an accident."

"I've been hearing sip sips that it may not be an accident after all," he whispered. "Some people believe she's been murdered."

"Murdered?" I whispered back. "That's impossible and utterly ridiculous to even conceive!"

He quickly tapped my arm to remind me to keep the volume down.

"I surely hope that's not the case!" I said. "I really can't afford to see another ghost!"

"You see ghosts?" He looked surprised.

Merlene's famous scratched record played again inside my head: *"Lucille, you talk too much!"*

"Just kidding." I decided to end the subject there. But the expression on his face was: *Kidding? Really? At a time like this?*

I don't know why people just don't learn to pardon people my age. Frankly, I think we've lived long enough to say whatever the hell we want.

This Lance fellow seemed to take charge of this so-called group interrogation, while his partner and the Sheriff stood idly behind him. My living room had two tall, mahogany double doors that were usually kept ajar. Just before Lance Matthews commenced the interrogation, a uniformed police officer shut the doors. I was really so grateful to have the air-conditioning on because I shuddered to think what it would've been like stuck in that room in the heat with dozens of people releasing nothing but hot air and misery. I was miserable enough sometimes without a tragic accident or *murder* adding to it.

"I'm sure you all know why you're here, but for the record I'll say there's a young lady that died here tonight and our job here is to get to the bottom of it."

He seemed frank enough to me.

"I'd like to know if anyone actually saw with their own eyes what happened to Sabrina," he continued.

I thought it was a stupid question—the way he put it. Could anyone have seen what happened with anyone *else's* eyes? I'd think it would've had to be their own, but maybe it's just me.

Crickets could be heard in response to his question – literally.

"Well, we need to establish who last saw her and what she was doing before she fell to her death."

Jenny Barry, a neighbor from around the corner, cleared her throat. "I didn't want to say anything, but I think you should know. That lady got into an argument with a young man less than an hour or so before she was found dead."

All eyes were on Jenny. Many of the stares seemed to depict shock that she actually publicly made mention of that. This crew really was a joke if they thought no one would squeal.

"An argument? Where did it happen? On the balcony?" Lance asked.

"No. It was in here. They were standing right over there near the waterfall." She pointed. Jenny went on to explain what she'd witnessed.

"Who was she arguing with?"

Everyone was looking around the room, but I was more focused on Diane and Robert, the boys' parents. I didn't know if they were aware of what happened earlier since they'd been outside when the incident involving Sabrina and Brady occurred. They both had a nervous look on their faces.

"He's not here!" Jenny exclaimed. "He must've left. The guy who was with him also exchanged a few words with the lady and he's not here either."

"Is anyone able to identify who these two men are?" Sheriff Cooke interjected.

There was no immediate response, even though about half of the room, residents of Harriet's Cove, could have easily answered that question. I certainly wasn't going to be the one.

Robert Clover stood up moments later. "The young men she's referring to are our sons, Brady and Drake Clover," he said, rather unwillingly. "It's awful what happened here tonight and that a beautiful young woman lost her life, but I can assure you, Detectives… Sheriff… that Brady and Drake had nothing to do with it. They may be hard-headed and all, even biggity at times, but they're no killers." He paused, then sat down again.

Diane was sitting there looking petrified.

"Where are your boys, sir?" Lance asked.

"They're at home. They told us they were leaving because a girl had gotten mouthy or something and started attacking Brady. My older son, Drake, felt it was best in order to prevent his brother from getting in any kind of trouble."

"How long ago was this?" Lance asked.

"You mean—since they left?"

Lance nodded.

"About an hour ago, I think," Robert responded.

"Did anyone else see the young men leave?"

At least five or six people confirmed they saw the Clover boys head out.

Sheriff Cooke whispered something into Lance's ear, then went on his radio. I assumed he was arranging for someone to either pick up the boys or to question them at home.

"My wife and I decided to stay for Lucille's sake," Robert noted. "Young people disagree all the time, but most times, it doesn't escalate to anything." He quietly sat down again.

Carla Walkes stood up. "This might not mean anything… "she started rubbing her stubby fingers together nervously, "but while I was passing the staircase about fifteen minutes prior to the lady being discovered in the back yard, I saw that gentleman there," she pointed at David, "descend the stairs like he was in some sort of hurry. He looked really angry. Like I said, it might not mean anything." She took her seat.

David became the focus of everyone's attention and suddenly, his once constant sobbing ceased. He looked around the room as the eyes were darting away.

"Wait! I… I had nothing to do with Sabrina's death," he said. "Sure, we had a falling out, but it wasn't like I killed her because of it!" He turned to the detectives. "I basically told her I knew she didn't wanna be here and suggested she leave. As much as it hurt, I intended to walk away from the relationship tonight. There was no reason for me to kill her."

Sheriff Cooke stepped forward. "Accidents happen, son."

Even a fool knew what he meant. I was still appalled that Carla even brought that up. Didn't she know the guy was a tenant of mine? But I shouldn't have been surprised at all that the neighborhood number one gossiper was more than willing to sweeten the pot and rat someone out who she knew could be completely innocent.

There was no way those guys would've heard a word about David and Sabrina's argument from me, and I pretty much was like a fly on the wall when it took place. It would be silly of me to single out David when I knew the boy was as innocent as a kitty cat.

There was determined scratching at the double doors.

I stood up.

"Where are you going, Lucille?" Cooke asked.

"Am I the only one that hears my dog at the door?" I replied. "I'm going to get her."

"Mrs. Pfiffer," Lance started, "we cannot have an animal running around the room while we're conducting an interrogation."

"She won't be running around, Detective. I'm going to hold her."

"Now, ma'am, I won't permit that. The dog will remain outside of these doors until we've finished here."

I took my cane and continued on toward the door. Nilla's scratching intensified and now she was barking. I stopped all of a sudden and turned in the officers' direction. "First and foremost, Detective, let me remind you that this is *my* house! Vanilla is my pet and she needs me. You cannot and I repeat *cannot* stop me from tending to the needs of my pet!" I continued walking. I didn't know what their plan was at that point and I really didn't care. If they wanted to test me and see this old, blind woman fight anyone and their momma, this was the day. I felt for the handle and opened the double doors to my darn room. Nilla rushed to my feet and I quickly scooped her into my arms. She must've slipped away after I fell unconscious and hid under a chair.

"Let me help you back," Anthony offered.

Suddenly, the room erupted in applause and I realized they were mainly the members of the Pichton Pet Society who seemed elated by my supposed bravery. Nilla wagged her tail eagerly, I'm sure, feeling like she was the center of attention.

About midway back to my seat, my inner vision faded away and I really depended on Anthony then for guidance. Having a room full of chairs was not so easy for me to navigate through.

"Shall we carry on?" Lance asked after I'd taken my seat.

Nilla was licking my face and upper arm. It was her way of showing her love for me and also appreciation for ultimately getting what she wanted.

"What's your name?" Lance asked someone in the room.

"My name's David; David Bostwick."

"Where were you and Sabrina arguing?"

"We were in my bedroom upstairs."

"Which room is it?"

"The first one on the right side of the hallway," David replied.

There were a few moments of silence and then I heard Lance say, "If I'm correct, it was the balcony adjacent to your room where Sabrina toppled over."

Several guests made a collective gasp.

David was speechless. I could only imagine how troubled he was by all of this. First, losing his girlfriend *permanently*, with no chance at reconciliation and now being indirectly accused of murdering her.

"When you last saw Sabrina, was she alive?" Lance asked.

"'Course she was!" David exclaimed.

"Are you sure she didn't say something that caused you to lose control and you pushed her over the balcony?" It was the voice of Tyrone Stewart—the other detective who seemed to need a leash on his tongue.

"How dare you accuse my son of such an atrocity?" Merlene snarled. "I can put my head on a chopping block declaring his innocence. You all are barking up the wrong tree!"

I was proud of my girl. Only a heartless mother wouldn't stand up for her child, especially if she knew he was innocent.

At that moment, the darkness before me dissipated and faint images began to appear in front of and around me, which lingered for a few seconds more before I could solidly see everyone in the room again. I hoped my elation in this regard was not obvious. Merlene always said if I were foolish enough to tell anyone what often happened pertaining to this inner vision of mine either no one would believe me or if they did, they'd be sure I was a nutcase who practiced some sort of Black Magic. My reputation in Chadsworth would be ruined in my old age. Did I believe her? I guess I did, to some extent. If not, I'd probably have snitched on myself a long time ago.

"My! What an interesting conversation this is we're having!" Edna Haygood, the classy wife of Pichton Pet Society's Director stated. "Seeing the way things are obviously going, should I assume that *that* woman over there might've had something to do with Sabrina's death?" She briskly pointed at a middle-aged lady sitting near the back of the room. "A few minutes after the incident involving Sabrina and the young man, Brady, in this very room, that woman blatantly scolded Sabrina for the way she handled the man's advances; then she promptly walked away before Sabrina had a chance to respond." Edna spoke in a direct and dignified manner.

"Are you referring to me?" the woman asked in clear defense.

"Yes *you*!" Edna replied. "I am simply trying to make a point here though. Goodness knows how many other people in this room might've had an encounter with Sabrina before she fell to her death. Are we to assume that everyone who did is suspect in her murder—if it is, in fact, a *murder* we're dealing with here?"

Edna had a valid point and the lady she'd highlighted seemed to realize she wasn't actually accusing her of anything. I didn't recall seeing that woman Edna referred to arrive at the party, neither the lady who was sitting next to her. Maybe they were crashers or came with someone I was acquainted with. Freddie, Claire Fairweather's husband who sat a few chairs to the right of Edna, appeared somewhat agitated. I'd thought he certainly had good reason to be since the police had literally held all of us hostage.

“Wait a second, people,” an older man spoke up. “Why are we jumping to conclusions here? It’s quite logical that in spite of whatever arguments or disagreements took place, the girl simply lost her balance, for whatever reason after walking out onto the balcony, and fell over. It’s a rush of judgment, in my opinion, to assume that she was killed.”

“I agree with you,” Cooke addressed him. “We will wait for the completion of the forensic investigation and autopsy report, and from there we’ll know more of the facts. In the meantime, however, the purpose of us being here is to gather as much information as we possibly can that might help the case in the long run. We’re not jumping to any conclusions here; believe me. Just working to get the facts. And part of successfully conducting any investigation involves asking the tough questions.”

Sheriff Cooke made good sense, but the gentleman who spoke prior to him made even better sense, as far as I was concerned. From the way things were going, it sounded like they’d already pegged David in their minds as a suspect. Poor, sweet, harmless David.

11

Sheriff Cooke and his two stooges finally put an end to the *friendly* gathering where stinging accusations had been hurled about the room for the better part of an hour. Everyone cleared out and went their merry way.

Nilla, the boys and I had to go to a hotel until the forensic crew were finished with the house. David stayed with us the entire time, though he hardly left his hotel room even for a drink of water. He refused to go back home with his mother. Theodore and Anthony checked on him when they were not at work and even got him out at one time to play a game of Checkers. David mainly watched. He obviously couldn't muster the interest.

We returned home two nights later and met things pretty much intact. Theodore,

Anthony, Merlene and I talked for a while in the sitting room, as David mostly stood near the sliding door staring outside at where his beloved's body had been found. He was in a deeply somber mood.

"I'm really worried about him," Merlene said. "He hasn't been the same since…"

"I know," I replied. "What happened here was a shock to everyone."

"I can't believe that woman tried to accuse him of murder!" She whispered loudly. "Such gall she has!"

"Carla has a big mouth and a small brain," I said. "The woman doesn't know how to tame her tongue!"

Then again, I'm sure I'm guilty of the same thing. Anyway…Carla's on the hot seat right now. Not me.

Theodore leaned forward. "I think the whole thing was blown out of proportion. If those so-called detectives were anywhere near smart, they could've seen from the height of the balcony rail, Sabrina, being a fairly tall girl, could've fallen over by mistake if she somehow got distracted and wasn't paying attention to how close she was to it."

"I agree." Anthony nodded, glancing at David. "People are so quick to suspect the worse possible scenario. To think I went above and beyond to cater to some of those snakes that were at the party!"

"I'd say! We should've served rotten meat and venom to 'em!" I sighed. "This is the absolute worse thing that could've happened on our wedding anniversary. Donnie must be turning over in his grave."

Merlene patted my knee. "I'm sorry, Lucille. I think we've all forgotten amidst the chaos that it was your special day that was ruined too."

"I know it can't compare to someone losing their life, but thanks."

Merlene got up to check on David. "Why don't you come home with me tonight, sweetheart? I think it would be best if you didn't stay here," she said.

David slowly shook his head. "I wanna stay."

"But why? This can't be a healthy decision for you, considering what's happened."

"There you go again trying to control my life!" He yelled. "You think I'm gonna run home to you because of what happened? I guess you're glad she's dead, aren't you? Thinking you can have me all to yourself again."

"That's absurd, David and you know it!"

"I'm not a Momma's boy, Mom! I'm a grown man." He turned away again, looking out toward the yard. "I said I'm staying and that's final!"

Nilla shot past them and into the back yard, stopping where poor Sabrina's body had landed. She looked up toward the neighbor's house and started barking.

I went to get her. I had an awful feeling while approaching the spot where Nilla had chosen to stop at. I wondered if finding Sabrina there had traumatized her in any way. Holding her in my arms, I caressed her soft fur. "Come, sweet baby. It's way past your bedtime. Let's go inside now."

David walked off and sat outside on the back porch, less than ten feet away from where Sabrina's body landed.

Merlene joined us in the sitting room again.

"Give him time," I told her as she plonked down on the sofa. "He's really heartbroken right now."

"I know that, but how could he say I'm glad this tragedy happened? I don't understand how he could say that."

"I'm sure he didn't mean it," Anthony said. "Sometimes when we're upset, we say the cruelest things to each other and don't mean a word of it."

"I wish I could help him somehow. He's just in so much pain," she said.

Merlene was having a tough time herself, watching David, whose welfare was her ultimate concern. She'd move mountains for that boy and that's no understatement.

After she left for the night, David went up to his room, while Theodore and Anthony started cleaning up the place. I thought it was remarkable that David had offered to help, despite what he was going through, but the boys quickly declined his offer and encouraged him to get some rest. I was impressed by my boys. Yes, they were *my* boys now—my family. I always said that family has nothing to do with blood flowing through the veins, but everything to do with love and compassion inside the heart—a willingness to look out for each other, come Hell or high water.

After putting Nilla on her favorite side of the bed, I walked out into the hallway, deciding to check on David. His door was shut and I could tell the room was in complete darkness. Knocking softly, I said, "David… can I come in?"

Moments later, the door creaked open.

"Yeah," he said, dryly, flipping on the light switch at the door.

"Are you all right?"

He walked off and sat down on the bed. "You wanna sit down?" he asked.

He told me where he was, just in case I couldn't see him, and I went and sat next to him.

"I know I've said this before, but I really am truly sorry about what happened to Sabrina," I said.

"Thanks." He lowered his head and looked like he'd lived a thousand lives.

"I want you to know that no one here believes you're in any way responsible for her death, no matter what anyone in that meeting alluded to. The whole thing was just an accident and the law enforcement goons and everyone else will soon realize that."

"I don't care what they think! I know I didn't do anything." He slid his hands across his cheeks.

"That's the spirit!"

I squeezed his shoulder, then got up to leave.

"Are you sure you want to stay here tonight, David?" I could see the balcony a few feet off where Sabrina toppled over. "Your mother did have a point, you know, and I'm sure it came from a purely unselfish heart."

"The last words I said to Sabrina were right in this room, Miss Lucille," he replied, softly. "They were harsh because I was angry. I can't just leave and not somehow make amends."

"I understand."

At least I *thought* I understood. I knew we'd have to keep an eye on this young man, especially considering those words could mean just about anything.

After I'd freshened up for bed, I encouraged Theodore and Anthony to leave the cleaning up for the next day. They must've been exhausted already anyway, but I don't think they took my advice.

I stretched out next to Nilla, whose favorite night-time spot was on the fluffy, pink mat next to my bed. Tonight, however, I felt she needed to be closer to me and I to her. A beautiful, young girl had died on these premises the night of my and Donnie's anniversary, and for everyone, I tried to put up a brave facade, but inside, Lucille Velma Abigail Pfiffer was completely horrified.

12

In the middle of the night, I awoke to a strange sound, as if someone had loudly whispered into my ear. I felt for Nilla, but soon realized she'd left my soft mattress, presumably for her preferred spot.

I sat up in bed as an explosion of bright light surrounded me. Standing in my room at the foot of my bed was none other than Sir Clement. I was beginning to wonder how Donnie felt about this fine man appearing constantly to his wife and if there was any jealousy up there at all.

He gazed at me as if I was his Rapunzel—without the hair.

"What do you want?" I asked. "What do any of you want? Why do you come to me?"

It was the first time I'd ever asked and couldn't fathom why I'd never done so before. Maybe because their visits had often been few and far between, but I'd just seen the guy forty-eight hours ago and here he was again!

He didn't speak; only stared. Suddenly, on the left side of the glaring white light, I saw Sabrina crashing towards the hard earth from David's balcony. It was just her deadly flight I'd seen, then heard the thump which caused my heart to sink. Sir Clement's eyes reeked of something. I wondered if it was pain due to the fact that his own murder had never been solved. But why paint a picture of Sabrina falling from the balcony? Could it be that he was trying to tell me something? Could it be that she really might've been murdered, after all?

13

Sir Clement Tucker's most recent visit was stuck in my mind the moment I woke up the next morning. I knew within my heart of hearts that something wasn't right and for some reason, he wanted me to get to the bottom of it. It was also the first time I'd internally questioned, if even for a split second, if David might've had anything to do with his girlfriend's death. After all, they did have a heated argument shortly before the tragedy; I'd heard it with my own ears. But I also heard those footsteps leaving and descending the staircase after the argument. Would he have actually returned to commit the crime in the heat of passion?

No! I forced myself back to reality. There was no way my best friend's son could've done that. I'd known David since he was a little boy. He was the nicest, gentlest child a parent could have. Merlene had always spoken of the gentle nature of her son and she feared it's what the wrong type of woman in his life would've preyed upon. Perhaps, her fears were realized in Sabrina, though I never heard a good enough reason why she doubted the girl's sincerity and professed love for David. I'd always chalked it up to her being overly-protective and *Miss Bossy* as she often was with me.

That morning, Nilla and I went for our usual stroll around the neighborhood. As people were out and about or on their way to work, we, as expected, were the center of attention. Well, I always liked attention, so they were really doing a wonderful deed. I was lucky to have had clear inner vision and was *allowed* to see some of the beauty of nature.

On our way back, we stopped by a narrow stream on the eastern end of the subdivision. Nilla went toward the water's edge and stuck her little tongue out to the water. She didn't drink it though. Never once did, but it did seem that one taste wasn't enough for her. Every time we passed that way, she'd stick her tongue into the water, then turn away.

The glistening stream traveled from one end of our neighborhood and into the ocean. Schools of tiny, silver fish could be seen and

Nilla found them most fascinating. She'd stand and bark at them as if they were tiny intruders. I loved it there and often used it as a time to reflect, whether I could see anything or if nothing but darkness stood within my view. That day was as good as any to reflect. This time, it was on Sabrina's death and how her reluctance to show up at the party had affected everyone present. She'd surely made an indelible imprint in my life by choosing to die on my property.

We remained near the stream for a few minutes, then headed home. As we approached the Andersons who lived next door, a woman I'd never seen before was dumping a trash bag into their outside bin.

"Hi There!" I said.

She looked startled. I think it was obvious to her that I was blind. There I went slipping up again; I guess some people never learn. Nilla instantly started barking at her and dashing around erratically, which was rather odd since she usually just sniffed at and quietly, but seriously analyzed strangers.

"Hi," she replied.

It appeared she was in rush to get away.

"Don't worry. She won't bite you as long as I hold this leash tight enough."

"Okay, I am going back inside now."

She hurried up the walkway and entered the house. I assumed she was the Andersons' new housekeeper. She'd spoken with an accent which I thought sounded Hispanic, especially since she looked Hispanic, but I could be mistaken.

Debbie's white sedan was in the yard. I thought of giving her a hail as we'd only spoken once since the tragedy. But felt I'd better get home as soon as possible before I had an *accident* outside on the sidewalk—the type of accidents Nilla occasionally had in my house. Admittedly, she's not as bad with it as she was when she was a pup. Those days, any and everywhere was her bathroom. But nowadays, she holds it quite well until she gets outside and bugs me when it seemed I've lost track of time after she's had her meal. Just once in a blue moon she might decide, *Who cares!* And lets it out anywhere. And usually, the scent is strong enough to guide me to where it is without a need for vision.

As soon as we got into the house, I went upstairs as quickly as I could and locked Nilla out of the bathroom. That was my private time. I was sure she could find one of my shoes to continue chewing on for the time being.

A minute later, the phone rang, which I ignored. Then there was a knock at the door.

"Miss Lucille, phone's for you," David said.

"Can't it wait? I'm busy now."

"It's Debbie from next door. She says it's important."

David had taken a few days off work for what was called "emergency vacation". I thought it was the best thing for him to do, considering the circumstances. I quickly got myself together, washed my hands and opened the door. He handed me the phone and returned to his room.

"Lucille…" Debbie started. "I didn't want to mention anything to David although this concerns him. I felt you'd be able to prepare him if I told you first."

"Uh huh… What is it?" I asked.

"A friend of mine, Shelly Cambridge, who works for the Sheriff's Department, just called and said they're on their way to pick David up." She spoke passionately.

"For what?" I could feel my heart beginning to race.

"You know…"

"My goodness. What could they possibly have to be able to do that?" I spoke as quietly as I could. "Did Shelly say anything else?"

"No. That's all she told me. They're gonna be there at any minute now, so you'd better warn David."

I hung up and immediately called David.

"What's up?" He asked.

"The Sheriff…they're coming to arrest you, David." I felt my otherwise strong lips trembling.

"What?! Why?" He held his head in frustration.

I sighed. "I guess it has to do with Sabrina's death. Don't panic though. Just keep it together. They can't possibly have actual evidence that you've done anything to harm her."

I could see my words had barely gotten through to him because he was obviously in a full blown panic. Suddenly, I heard the front door creak open and close.

"Lucille! Are you home?" Merlene cried.

"We're upstairs!" I hollered back.

David took off downstairs to his mother.

"Miss Lucille said they're coming to arrest me, Mom. They're coming to arrest me!"

Merlene's eyes widened with shock and terror. She looked at me as I descended the staircase. "Lucille…"

"Debbie just called," I said. "Someone at the Sheriff's office tipped her off."

"My God! They can't be serious. How can they think they can come here and arrest him without any evidence that he killed that girl?"

"*Sabrina,* Mom," David said defensively. "Her name was Sabrina."

"I'm sorry, David. I didn't mean to…"

"Forget it. I guess I'll be one of those guys they lock up and throw away the key on—who'll be serving time for the rest of my life for a crime I didn't commit."

Merlene hugged her son. Ironically, for the first time since he'd left their home, I could tell she actually felt she was needed again. It was a shame it had to happen at a time like this.

When I made it down the stairs, there was a loud knock at my front door.

Merlene stayed with David while I headed to the door. On the other side were Sheriff Cooke, Detective Lance Matthews, and two uniformed officers. Loud mouth Stewart wasn't with them. Was probably injured due to a shooting off at the mouth.

"Lucille, it's Sheriff Cooke and Detective Matthews…" Cooke said.

"Thanks for the intro, but I know who's standing in front of me." I didn't give a rat's behind about being discreet at that point. I was only concerned about David.

"Is David Bostwick here?" Cooke asked.

"What's it to you?"

"We have a warrant for his arrest."

"Based on what?" Merlene approached the door.

"May we come in, Lucille?" Cooke practically ignored Merlene. "I don't want us to have to force our way through."

I stepped aside.

"You put your hands on my son and I'll kill you!" Merlene growled.

Lance walked up to her. "Now I see where your son got that idea from to threaten people when he doesn't get his way."

"What the hell are you talking about?" Merlene didn't blink.

"I can take what you said as a threat, Miss Bostwick and have you thrown in the slammer. Just watch yourself."

"And you watch how you're speaking to my mother!" David yelled.

One of the uniformed officers proceeded to cuff him.

"David Bostwick, we have a warrant for your arrest for the murder of Sabrina Abrams," Cooke said. And he proceeded to read him his Miranda Rights.

"On what grounds are you arresting him?" I asked.

"Take him!" Cooke told the officers.

As they escorted David outside, Lance joined them and Merlene was on their heel, hollering at them and accusing them of trying to railroad her son. I'd never seen her so angry.

As the Sheriff started to leave, I put my hand on his arm.

"Sheriff, what do you have on this young man?" I asked.

"Lucille, you should know I can't disclose that information right now."

"I think if you arrest someone publicly, I…the *public* have a right to know why you're arresting him."

"We're taking him in to confront him with serious evidence we came across. It was enough to have a warrant issued for his arrest." He'd lowered his voice. "I have to go."

"Sheriff…"

"Yes, Lucille!" He was obviously becoming a bit impatient with me, but I knew he only gave me the time of day because of my disability and I'd known the man practically all of his life.

"No matter what you found, I *know* David and I know he hasn't done what you're accusing him of. One way or the other I'm going to get to the bottom of this and you'll see that I'm right."

"Now, you leave the investigating to the professionals, ya hear? Furthermore, what do you think you can do to prove anything?"

If I hadn't known the guy well enough to realize he hadn't insulted me over the fact that I'm blind, I would've given him a good one right across the face—law man or not.

"Lucille, I didn't mean…"

He'd realized after-the-fact how his remark sounded.

"I know," I replied. "But mark my words… I mean exactly what I said."

He shook his head as he walked out of the house. As the two squad cars pulled away, Merlene was about to hop into her Toyota.

"Where are you going?" I shouted.

"To the Sheriff's Department. Where else?"

"Wait for me. I'm coming!"

I went to check on Nilla, but she was upstairs in Theodore's room the entire time the commotion had taken place. Apparently, she'd found his shoes, especially the ones with laces, far more interesting to explore.

Her favorite gourmet food and a fresh bowl of water was left at the foot of the stairs for her, and I headed out with Merlene to the Sheriff's office.

14

"What took you so long?" Merlene snapped at me.

"Had to check on Nilla. I was moving as quickly as I could!"

She didn't respond and I could not only see, but feel the tension all around her.

"He's going to be all right," I said. "Despite what they think they have, I know they're only grasping at straws."

I went on to share with her the brief conversation I had with Cooke and she called his claim of them having serious evidence *hogwash.*

I was standing with her and David all the way. Maybe Cooke *thought* they had something, but I highly doubted it was anything sustainable when it really came down to having hard physical evidence in place.

We waited for Cooke and his goons to interrogate David for the better part of three hours before Cooke and Lance re-surfaced, and to my dismay hard-nosed Stewart. David was led out in handcuffs into the corridor and Merlene and I hurried over to him. Merlene had me by a good ten seconds because by the time I got up out of my chair, she was already reaching for her son. The officer accompanying him stopped her.

"Where are you taking him?" she demanded.

"He'll be in a holding cell, Miss."

Merlene reached again for David. And the officer used his right arm as a barrier.

"Can't you allow a mother to hug her child, you big brute of a man?" I said, behind them.

He gave me a similar look to that of the strange woman I'd seen in the Andersons' front yard.

He eyed my cane at least twice before saying, "Miss, can I ask you something?"

"Am I holding your tongue?" I replied, sharply. By then, I was annoyed at the whole situation—them coming and arresting David, and now holding him there as if he's some common criminal. When I got to that point of anger, my tongue held no evidence of ever being tamed.

"Aren't you blind?"

"What do you think? You think I'm holding this white cane for no reason? Of course, I am!"

"Well, how do you…"

"Thompson!" Another officer yelled his way. "Take the prisoner to the cell!"

The baffled guy heeded his colleague's demand and continued on, taking David to an area where a large, red sign hung on the wall that read: *Authorized Personnel Only*.

"Don't worry about anything, honey! I'll get you the best attorney money can buy and you'll be out of here in no time!"

David just nodded.

The officer did look back at me one last time before they disappeared through the double doors ahead. I must admit I took pleasure in getting him all confused like that. What kind of officer won't allow a heartbroken mother to embrace her son? The nerve of that guy!

I took Merlene's hand as she angrily wiped away her tears. I knew it tore her to pieces to see her precious David handled like a criminal.

"Merlene…" A voice crept up behind us. It was Detective Lance Matthews.

"Why are you keeping David here?" She quickly confronted him.

"Can I see you in my office a minute?"

He then looked at me as if there was something on his mind, but I knew Merlene had picked up.

"She's coming with me," she said.

Lance cleared his throat. "That's no problem. No problem at all."

We followed him in the same direction David was taken where the large, red sign was. Lance's office was the last one on the right of a long, narrow hallway.

He helped me to my seat on the *visiting side* of a small pine desk and Merlene sat next to me. Resting his arms on the desk, he interlaced his fingers and said, "The reason I asked you in here is give you a brief update as to what we're looking at concerning David."

"Please do!" Merlene exclaimed, positioning herself further to the edge of her chair.

Lance sighed deeply. "We've uncovered evidence, though circumstantial, that David had publicly threatened to kill Sabrina just two days prior to her death."

"What?" Merlene arched her brow. "Is that what you used to get a warrant to arrest my son? People make threats all the time when they're angry. It doesn't mean that they intend to follow through with any of it." She looked at me, shaking her head. "I can't believe a judge actually issued a warrant based on hearsay!"

"Eyewitness testimony is very powerful," Lance replied. "We've seen many convictions based on them."

"So that's all you've got?" I asked, just to make sure.

"I'm afraid not. We were able to secure text messages over a period of months between the two and it's evident that they were having relationship issues. I cannot go into any details concerning those messages, but I *can* say it doesn't look good for David."

"Text messages?" Merlene grimaced. "Relationship issues? Who doesn't have them? I presume none of those text messages are actual documented death threats like you claimed David made publicly against Sabrina, or you would have said that. Am I right?"

Lance slid his hands away the desk. "As I said, I can't get into the actual details of those messages. My appeal to you is to speak with David and let him understand, like we tried to, that it would be more beneficial to him in the long run to come out and confess to what he might have done. That way, the court will be a bit more lenient when it comes down to sentencing."

"That's a load of crap!" I blurted, almost vomiting up the bile of nonsense he just spewed out. "You really don't care if the young man you've got back there is guilty or innocent; you just think you've got a nicely wrapped, neat pile of circumstantial evidence that really in my mind amounts to the clear fact that you've got nothing."

"I second that!" Merlene said. She leaned in a bit more. "Have you people even bothered to check out those Clover boys who caused that upset at Lucille's party that night, instead of trying to pin murder charges on David just because he was in a relationship with that girl?"

"The Clover boys have been cleared, Merlene," Lance said. "Multiple sources verified that both boys left the party right after the incident."

"Either of them could've returned, in my estimation, and they could've gone unnoticed."

"That's highly improbable."

"That's where you're wrong," she replied. "There were about fifty of sixty people at the party. Many were outside under the tent and others were in the living room. Anyone could've entered through a clearing which leads to Lucille's back yard, hopped the fence and eased in through the sliding door which was left open practically the entire night. Then they could've taken the flight of stairs up to David's room and pushed Sabrina off the balcony."

"How would your suspect have known Sabrina was on the balcony or upstairs there to begin with?" he asked.

"They could've seen her when they were approaching the yard through the clearing and quietly hopped the fence at an angle where she wouldn't have noticed them," Merlene explained.

"It also could've been an accident," I chimed in. "No murder had to have taken place at all."

You're right!" Merlene agreed. "I think the police have blown this whole thing out of proportion and skewed everyone's thinking in the house that night during the questioning."

Lance's glare was set on Merlene. "We had nothing to do with skewing anyone's thinking. Don't forget, it was one of the guests who implied that something might've gone awry when she filled us in on the incident."

"That person volunteered that tidbit because she knew that's the type of information the police would be looking for," I said." "There was already sip sip about the fall being more than it appeared to be, so naturally, she added more flame to the fire because some people are actually excited by that sort of thing."

"I just wanna know how long you plan on keeping David here," Merlene said.

"We have a forty-eight hour window, then we'll decide if we're going to turn things over to the Prosecutor's Office.

"That's considering you find something to stick before those forty-eight hours are up," I noted. "I know how this thing works."

Lance didn't reply.

Merlene reached for my hand and stood up. "Let's go, Lucille! All this jerk has done was waste our time."

Lance stood as well. "Maybe we should be investigating *you*," he said.

Merlene looked back. "What do you mean by that, Detective?"

He shoved his hands into his pockets. "I heard you couldn't stand Sabrina. In fact, by all accounts, you hated her. Maybe you hated her enough to murder her that night. After all, you had clear access to David's room and the balcony. You could be the killer and maybe David truly is innocent."

"How dare..." I started before Merlene cut me off.

"That's okay, Lucille," she said. "I got this."

She put her hands on his desk, leaned over and said, "I wish you would arrest me and let my son go. By the time I get through with you, I'd make this Department the laughing stock of Chadsworth. And when it's said and done, whether it's me you victimize or my son you continue to victimize, the state will pay one way or the other and there will be no mercy."

"Is that another threat, Merlene? You're really good at those," he replied.

"You bet it is. I'm not afraid of the slammer and I'm not afraid of an amateur kid like you. I'm old enough to be your mother. You wanna play ball? Let's play!"

I must admit, Lance looked quite surprised by Merlene's response. Not sure what he was expecting, but my girl doesn't play around. Merlene's extra threat ended the conversation right there. We passed Sheriff Cooke on our way to the exit. He'd been speaking with an officer in the reception area.

"Lucille… Merlene..." he started.

"Shut up, tubby! "Merlene barked, stopping for a minute. "You've got my son for the time being, but I'm gonna make sure this department full of nincompoops will be hanging from the rafters by the balls!"

"You handled yourself really well, Merlene. I'm proud of you," I said, as we drove off.

"You did too," she replied, as the tears began to flow again.

"Tell you what… go see Mickey Carey at *Carey, Jacques and Bledsoe*. He's the best of the best. Tell him I sent you to get David out of jail and off the hook."

"Mickey Carey? I can't afford him. My house isn't even valued enough to use as collateral to pay that guy!"

"You did tell David you're going to get the best attorney."

"Yes, but I meant..."

I rested my hand on her shoulder. "Merlene, I know you don't have the money to afford a good lawyer, but I do."

Her tears flowed even more as the implication of my words set in.

"You've got to stop crying though because your make up is all messy and you're starting to look like a clown."

That got her laughing.

"That's better."

"Lucille..."

"Think nothing of it," I said.

"Are you sure you can afford to do that? I don't see where I'd ever be able to pay you back, unless I come over and clean your house from top to bottom a couple of times a week for the rest of my life."

"Sounds like a plan." Then, I realized Merlene could be slow at times. "Just kidding. Look, Merlene… you don't have to pay me back—ever. David's just like my own son."

That's very generous of you." She glanced my way. "But how can you afford it? You depend a lot on your disability checks and it's not like you charge all that much for your rented rooms."

"Donnie's insurance money – a half a million dollars' worth."

"What?" Her eyes widened with shock.

"Yup. I never touched a dime of it since he died because we had pretty good savings. Before I started renting the rooms, I was living off a small portion of our savings and my disability checks. I know I never told you because finances was something we rarely ever discussed and you never asked. But we've been friends for a long time and I trust you to keep this confidential. I've told no one else about the insurance money," I said.

"My lips are sealed. I just can't believe you'd do this for us."

"Not for *us*," I emphasized. "For David. I don't see *you* behind bars." I got her to laugh again. By this time, she was drying her tears with an old towel she kept in the car. She'd wash it whenever it got soiled, then return it to its rightful place.

Gratitude oozed from her pores and it was rather uncomfortable for me, though I appreciated it. Yet, anymore of it was about to get me aggravated. I was never the *mushy* type and Merlene knew that better than anybody. She wasn't either, except with David—her pride and joy.

"Take me home. Nilla's probably wondering if I skipped town," I told her. "Go on to Mickey's office and don't leave 'til you see him. Let him know I'm taking care of the bill. He and Donnie were good friends, so I assume he knows I won't double-cross him."

She dropped me off approximately twenty minutes later and I walked into a quiet house. The boys were still at work and I found Nilla fast asleep in front of the sliding door which leads out back. I thought it strange since she'd always headed under the sofa for naps, but she must've been really exhausted from pulling out all of my shoes from the downstairs closet. I'd made the mistake, while rushing out to catch Merlene, of not ensuring the closet door was completely shut before leaving. Nilla obviously had a field day in there as my shoes were dragged all over the living room.

In the solitude of the moment was when I realized that for the entire day I didn't experience any fading of inner vision and could see everything clearly. I couldn't help but wonder if Sir Clement's visit the night before might've had anything to do with it since it was certainly unlike any of his former appearances. At first, the thought seemed absurd, but I quickly recalled his first ever visit was during Donnie's heart attack and it was then that my inner vision was ignited. Could he possibly have anything to do, by some celestial appointment, with the gift of my inner sight? If the profound possibility even existed, the question would be *why*. What was so special about me and how come he keeps showing up? Why did *any* of them show up when Donnie was in trouble?

I could only hope that my good fortune of seeing would last, as it truly was my most precious and treasured commodity, apart from Nilla and Donnie's half a million, of course… and my disability checks.

Nilla's eyes popped open as I quietly approached her. I had a feeling she knew the instant I'd walked in and was just too tired to move at the time. It did happen once or twice before.

She ran toward me with what I called a "gallop", and as expected by her, I gave her my warmest embrace. Cuddling her was the best thing in the world.

"Let's go, Nilla." I set her down and got her leash. After attaching it, we headed outside.

She absolutely loved when we ventured outdoors together. In an instant, she'd muster up super dog vitality that was mainly reserved for our walks. However, I'd only intended our stroll that afternoon to be right next door to the Andersons.

We entered through the unlocked gate and followed the multi-colored pebbled walkway which led to their front door. Debbie and Gary had done a marvelous job with that house after they'd moved in. For years, it had been owned by a wealthy widow named Sophia Cassidy who lived well below her means in hopes of hoarding as much money as she possibly could to take with her in the plain, pine casket she ultimately went off in. Apparently, her brother Clive and sole heir to her estate, since she was childless, saw the need to bury her in the most economical way, so there'd be plenty of millions left for him and his family's bad spending habits. I was determined not to go down like Sophia, though my finances were *chump change* compared to what she'd inherited from her late husband, Jack's oil company, before she sold it to some tycoon for double its worth.

The Andersons' two-storey house was a light brown shade with two sets of tall, white, fluted columns in front. The tiled roof shingles further accentuated the beauty of the house, giving it an imperial look.

We stepped onto the porch and Nilla browsed and sniffed around the eastern corners and about. I pressed the doorbell.

Shortly thereafter, the front door swung open.

"Lucille! Please come in," Debbie said.

She looked lovely in that pink and white cotton pants outfit she wore with dangling, white pearl earrings to match. I never saw her hair in a ponytail; always looked like she'd just stepped out of a salon. How she managed that, I have no clue. Maybe she had something against ponytails. They surely worked for me when I kept my hair long enough to pull into one.

Nilla and I stepped onto the shiny floor of the spacious living room. The place, as usual, was immaculate. For Debbie, it could be no other way. Gary once told me he thought she might be battling OCD, but to me, Debbie was just plain neat and tidy—in her appearance and her surroundings. I never understood why people think we need a special name for not being a slob.

Debbie was a frequenter of cruise ships and collected antiques from all over the world which now sat on the center and side tables of the room. There were at least fifteen in all, but I was sure more were in other parts of the house as well. Water globes, ceramic dolls—some which looked rather spooky, the likes of which I'd never let into my house—religious relics, etc.

"Nilla!" She stooped down and patted my girl's silky fur. Yes, I say that with pride. Nilla's tail wagged wildly. She liked Debbie a lot.

After offering me a seat and giving Nilla permission to roam about the floor, she asked, "How did it go today?"

"Not so good," I said. "They haven't released David and Merlene is beside herself." I filled her in on everything.

"In your heart of hearts, do you really think he's innocent?" she asked.

"Yes." I nodded. "David's a good boy."

"I don't have an opinion about his guilt or innocence, Lucille, but I just hope when it's all said and done—when the truth comes out—David would've lived up to your expectations."

That was my hope as well, particularly since my faith in him could cost me a pretty penny with Mickey on the case. But I didn't tell her that.

A short time later, the lady I'd seen in the Andersons' front yard the other day entered the room with a black shoulder bag. Nilla, who'd been busy chewing the edge of Debbie's Oriental living room rug, immediately turned and started barking at the woman, as if she were a fierce enemy.

"Good afternoon," she said, glancing my way, as she kept a good eye on Nilla, who was advancing toward her, then backing away, then advancing again. She was often suspicious whenever strangers came to my house, but she was going overboard a bit here. Perhaps, in that moment she'd forgotten she was in Debbie's house and not ours. *Nope!* Nilla could just get biggity at times and appoint herself the boss of other people's domains.

I hailed back.

"Nilla! Settle down!" I cried.

By then, Debbie had reached down and put her on her lap, but that did nothing to stop the barking.

"Mrs. Anderson, I'm going to leave now, if you don't mind," she said. "I've finished the kitchen cupboards, as you requested."

"Thank you, Angela," Debbie replied. "Before you go, I'd like to introduce to you my next door neighbor, Lucille, and her puppy, Vanilla."

"It's very nice to meet you again, Miss Lucille."

"Again?" Debbie glanced at us both. "You two already met?"

"Yes, at the end of the yard when I was emptying the trash the other day," Angela said.

"Yes indeed," I affirmed. "I figured you were the newest addition to the Anderson family."

Angela appeared slightly confused by the remark.

"I figured you were the new housekeeper," I clarified. Didn't want her to think I was insulting her.

"Yes! Yes!" she smiled.

"Angela's working out quite well," Debbie remarked, much to the woman's obvious satisfaction.

"Nilla! Have some manners!" I yelled. She would not stop her barking.

"Well, I'd better be on my way." Angela grinned nervously. "It was nice meeting you, Miss Lucille."

"It was wonderful meeting you too, Angela."

Nilla and I returned home shortly after Angela had left. I couldn't understand Nilla's harsh reaction both times to Angela, but I guess she had her reasons. Maybe she just didn't like her.

I spent the remainder of the afternoon analyzing what I'd learned and trying to figure out how I would possibly get David out of this mess. Mickey Carey called around 6:00 p.m. for me to verify Merlene's claim that I'd take care of the bill. He knew I was good for it, but he also knew I was no fool when it came to my money.

He'd have to work his butt off for whatever was coming his way financially. The plan was for him to see David the next day and work on compiling enough information to plant doubt into any potential juror's mind should the case go to court. Sounded good, but I wasn't about to put David's life—hook, line and sinker—in the hands of any lawyer; the stakes were just too high for that. At least with Mickey on the case, Merlene could have peace of mind, to some extent. My peace would only come when I'd dug into every ditch that held clear evidence of David's innocence.

Sir Clement showed up in my room later that evening looking as stunning as ever. This time, he came bearing a gift. Of all things—a phone book.

With arms extended with the thick directory in hand, I said, "What's this?"

I reached for it, but it fell through my hands, then disappeared.

"Why don't you ever speak?" I frowned. "In the movies, some ghosts actually speak to people. What's wrong with you?"

His eyes caught something on the bed, and I saw the phone book again, spread wide open in front of me. Lines and lines of names and their corresponding numbers didn't bring me any closer to what he wanted to convey to me. "What?" I hoped Sir Clement would simply explain. Then, in a flash, the book was gone and he just stared. I really couldn't be bothered.

Standing quietly at the foot of my bed, Sir Clement kept me company for a few more minutes before I pushed everything, except Nilla aside, and decided to go to sleep.

15

Theodore's car was a Mustang—fast and furious—and he kept it in spotless condition, especially with that fresh new coat of shiny, blue paint it got two weeks earlier. Theodore drove with an air of confidence and style as we headed to Pichton Pet Society's second meeting of the month.

Nilla was in the backseat and quiet during the entire drive. Vehicular movement used to make her very nervous when she was younger, but the fear subsided over time.

"Thanks for coming with me," I told Theodore. It was his day off and to think he chose to spend part of it with me, along with a group of Merlene's *favorite* people was commendable. At any other time, I could have joked about that with Merlene, but understandably, she wasn't in the very best mood as of late.

Theodore pulled into the parking lot of the Recreation Center on the Pichton property. Regular meetings were supposedly held there as opposed to where I'd attended the week before.

It was a large oval shaped facility with glass panels encircling the exterior. The moment we stepped inside, I understood why they called it the Recreation Center. The interior was sectioned off with dogs in one area—smaller and larger ones were further separated. Cats were in another area, caged birds and even snakes. Yes, *snakes*! There were toys for all the animals, fun mazes for them to play in and lots of other forms of entertainment. It was Animal Disneyland and I must admit, I was extremely impressed. To build and then run such a place was no cheap venture and I realized why so many high-society folks were involved. If I hadn't already thought well of myself, I'd have probably felt like I wouldn't have belonged there, even though nothing was ever too good for my Nilla.

She barked excitedly as she checked out a few of the other Shih Tzu that showed up with their owners and three Poodles that obviously found her quite interesting. Everyone seemed to be sniffing each other; I wondered what they all smelled. Nilla got to explore one of the mazes and Theodore laughed heartily as she seemed to be confused about midway as to which direction to take. He tried to coach her, but I don't think she trusted Theodore to lead her in the right direction, especially after she knew she was responsible for biting those toes of his countless times. Theodore must've thought for a moment before volunteering his help that *revenge is sweet!*

"Lucille, I'm so glad you came!" Claire Fairweather approached our booth.

"It's great to be here, Claire," I said. It's good that we were now on a first name basis.

She took my hand and led me aside. "How have you been keeping since the awful tragedy that night? We all thought what took place was horrible and it's a shame it happened on your anniversary."

"Yes, quite a shame."

"Everything was going so well before that; we were all enjoying ourselves so much and then that happened. I wondered why that young lady ever came in the first place. She brought bad energy into the room the moment she showed up—not that she deserved such a fate, of course."

Nodding, I replied, "Bad energy, for sure."

I noticed her husband, Freddie, in the kitty section with some other people, looking my way a couple of times, but everytime I caught his stare, he turned away. *Odd.* I wouldn't have thought he was at my party eating his belly full several nights ago if I hadn't seen it with my own mind. I wondered where his manners ran off to. Montey Williams joined us in the middle of the discussion and he expressed his dismay regarding the incident.

They'd both heard of David's arrest and clearly reserved their feelings pertaining to his guilt or innocence.

Eventually, within the hour and a half we spent there, everyone who was at the party that night came over to say hello. Everyone except, Jim Haygood, who was attending a Pet Welfare conference outside of the city and Freddie Fairweather, who'd kept his distance from me the entire time.

16

As we drove back home, I pondered Sabrina's death and all the possibilities there were surrounding it. Then Sir Clement and that darn phone book he mentally accosted me with the night before popped into my head. "Take me to the phone company!" I said to Theodore, along Route 61. He had to make a swift U-turn a few yards up. The car skidded, then glided like it was on thin air. It was obvious Theodore hadn't gotten his license through the *back door*; he really knew how to drive!

Nilla had played herself into a comatose-like sleep after we'd left the Recreation Center. It was the first time she'd been around other dogs for quite some time. I always felt I had to protect her because she was so small.

I loved the concept of the Recreation Center and felt proud that day to be a part of something so dynamic, centered strictly around the welfare of animals. The years I'd spent with Nilla had given me a deep appreciation for all animals—even for the snakes some of the *weirdos* had brought along that day. The texture and hue of some of their skin, especially, the long, thick innocuous ones, was stunning. Of course, no one there knew that I could see anything other than darkness. They probably felt sorry for the blind, old lady who apparently couldn't appreciate any of the cool stuff that was going on. I giggled at their ignorance, yet was grateful that I hadn't been deprived. When I cared enough about being discreet, the protection of my disability checks were kept at the forefront of my mind.

"You're going to pay a bill or something?' Theodore asked after making the turn.

"I'm going to see someone," I replied. "A good friend."

He was quiet for a moment.

"Don't worry. I won't be dreadfully long." The need to assure him was evident, especially since he knew I was a talker. He probably shuddered at the thought that I'd rob him of an additional couple of hours he'd never get back.

"No problem at all, Miss Pfiffer."

Theodore was a good guy—very masculine, but gentle at the same time. One day, he'd make a lucky woman a wonderful husband.

He dropped me off at the front door while he parked further off in an available spot on the left side of the main entrance.

I assured him I knew my way around and as always, took my cane for guidance, which thankfully, I didn't really need at that point. Images were rolling across my mind like scenes on a TV screen. I saw the front door, people leaving and entering; and the security who greeted me warmly and asked if I needed assistance. He quickly went and got Glenda Risdal for me—the one person I'd come there to see.

"Lucille! How are you?" Glenda emerged shortly thereafter.

"I'm doing just fine, dear. And how are you? Lovely colors you've got on today."

Oops! Again.

"I swear, Lucille, if I didn't know you, I wouldn't think for a second that you didn't have twenty-twenty vision." She grinned.

"Is that your way of avoiding the word *blind,* my wonderful, considerate Glenda? I'm quite comfortable with it, you know. No need to waste words and syllables like *twenty-twenty*."

"You're too much, Lucille," she patted my shoulder. "What can I do for you today? Need to pay a bill?"

I sighed as I thought about what it was I really wanted and how much of a risk it would be for her if she obliged. "May I speak with you privately?" I asked.

"Sure. Let's go to my office."

We walked to her office situated just behind the payment counters that stretched across from one end of the room to the next. She shut the door and sat down after I was comfortably seated in the leather chair in front of her desk. Glenda was Manager of the local phone company and had spent the last two decades climbing the ladder from a customer service position all the way up to her current post. Throughout the years of my going there to take care of my phone bill, she'd shared with me her ups and downs, trials and triumphs. Her friendliness as a CSR in those early years and my loquaciousness as a customer are what connected us so well from the beginning.

"I suppose you heard what happened at my home several days ago," I started.

"I did. What an awful tragedy it was! To think, I would've been right there if I didn't happen to be travelling last weekend," she said.

"Yep. I suppose you also heard that they're holding David, Merlene's boy."

She nodded. "I heard that too. Do you think he killed that girl or was it just an accident?"

"He didn't kill her. Maybe no one did. But I'm trying to see what I can find out because right now, his freedom is at stake."

"What is it that you need, Lucille?" A more serious expression emerged on her face.

"I know what I'm about to ask you is putting your job on the line, but…"

"You wouldn't ask me if you didn't think it was really important," she interjected.

"Uh huh." I nodded.

"What is it?"

"I'd like a print-out of Sabrina Abram's phone record—calls, texts. She'd been dating David for the past six months and maybe something is there that can help his case somehow."

There were a few moments of silence while she obviously considered my request.

"Two detectives were in here the other day making the same request. Do you really think David is innocent?"

"I do. I truly do," I said.

"Well, that's enough for me."

She turned toward her computer and started typing.

"Thank you, Glenda. I really appreciate it."

"Don't mention it. Anything I can do to help."

A large printer sat in a corner of the office behind her desk. As the pages were shooting out, I could see all of the transactions—possibly hundreds of them listed on the sheets. That was the first time anything quite like that had happened to me, apart from the other night when I saw listings in the phone book Sir Clement had blatantly placed before me. Something was happening to me which affected my psyche even more and I was now becoming convinced that it had everything to do with this case. I was beginning to feel like it was a *calling* for me to set things straight somehow for David's sake. And even in some way for Sir Clement's sake, since he'd obviously given me a clue that there, in that building, was where I should be. Glenda got up and retrieved the pages, then sat down again.

From my mental picture of the print-out, I could tell from David's correspondence via text messages with Sabrina on May 9th, two weeks before her death, that he'd confronted her about possibly cheating on him and said if he ever found any proof of it, she'd live to regret it. Well, to me, that was the so-called details that Detective Lance said he couldn't disclose. A load of weak circumstantial evidence he'd used to try to get David to confess. The manner in which David had conducted himself while annoyed at Sabrina seemed contrary to his gentle nature, but maybe she'd brought out the worst in him. Nothing else about the text messages between the couple appeared to have spelt *murder*. But something else stood out to me and did so in grand fashion. I had to ask Glenda right away and like rather recently, I couldn't without possibly blowing my cover.

"What do you plan on doing with this Lucille, since…well, it's not like it's in braille."

I crinkled my forehead. "Glenda, did you look through the record at any point after the detectives came and requested a copy?"

"No. It didn't occur to me to do so. Why do you ask?"

"Whose number is 544-1661? You should see that listed dozens of times. It's not David's number."

"I can find out who it's registered to," she replied, looking through the report. "It could be a relative or somebody close to her. I guess it only can be, considering the number of times they've communicated within the past four months." She then looked at me. "Wait…how do you know about this number?"

I felt like I was a deer caught in headlights. I had to throw her off since my only concern right then was getting that information. "I'll explain later. Just please…find out whose number that is."

She returned to the computer again and in less than a minute, a red, rectangular block on her screen popped up.

"The number belongs to a Frederick Fairweather of Burrow's Heights," she revealed.

My heart sank. Suddenly, I had flashbacks of how nervous he appeared to be at my house during the group interrogation and then his odd behavior at the Recreation Center. I smelled a rat, for sure.

"Thank you, Glenda. Can I have that?"

"Sure!" She folded the print-out and tucked it into a white envelope, which I then transferred to my purse.

"Will you be all right?" I asked out of genuine concern.

"Do whatever you need to do with the print-out, Lucille. Don't worry about me. I've got too much dirt on the powers that be for them to even think of bothering me if *the you know what hits the fan*. My job here is secure."

I smiled with relief.

Glenda and I embraced before she walked with me out toward the exit.

Theodore and Nilla were waiting in the air-conditioned foyer. Nilla was comfortably stretched across his lap.

"I hope I didn't keep you waiting for too long," I said to Theodore.

"Twenty minutes wasn't such a long time." He stood up. "Wanna go down to Frank's Grub and grab some lunch?"

"Sure, why not?"

I felt especially good knowing I'd discovered something that the police had obviously chosen to overlook. What their reasoning was, I'd find out sooner or later.

17

The next morning, I showed up at Debbie Anderson's door, alone. I'd barely slept the night before due to the constant flashbacks that flooded my mind. Scenes from the party—greeting guests at the door; Frederick Fairweather's suspicious behavior, Sir Clement and the others encircling Sabrina's dead body on the ground in my back yard; the print-out from the phone company.

"Hi, Lucille," Debbie answered the door. Judy was close by in the living room.

"Good morning, Miss Pfiffer!" Judy exclaimed.

I always appreciated the child's cheerful demeanor. Angela, the housekeeper, entered the adjacent dining room with a broom and dustpan in hand.

"Good morning, everyone," I said. "Sorry to be coming by so early."

"That's all right, Lucille." Debbie invited me in.

I went inside, but declined her offer to sit down. Gary hurried down the stairs, gave me a quick hail, then was out the door. Always on the go—the story of his life.

"I came to see Angela," I said.

Debbie looked confused.

"Me?" Angela stopped her sweeping.

"Judy, can you excuse us for a few minutes?" I asked.

"Okay!" She immediately dashed up the stairs.

"She's gone," Debbie advised. "What is it that you need to see Angela about, Lucille?"

"Debbie, remember at the party after you all arrived, you mentioned your housekeeper had forgotten her purse and you left the door unlocked for her to enter and get it?"

"Yes, I remember."

"What time did you arrive back at the house, Angela?" I asked.

She suddenly seemed nervous. "A…A little after eight o'clock, maybe."

"Did you go up to the balcony that night for any reason? The one that overlooks my back yard?"

"No!" she quickly retorted. "I never went out to the balcony that night. I got my purse and left."

I slowly approached her. "Tell the truth, Angela. It's very important."

"I *am* telling the truth!" She looked Debbie's way for support.

"Why are you afraid, Angela?"

"Lucille, what is this about?" Debbie asked.

"Angela knows who killed Sabrina. Yes, I said *killed*."

Debbie was aghast.

"Someone pushed her over the rail and your housekeeper here witnessed it."

"That's not true! She's a liar!" Angela shouted.

"You know I'm telling the truth," I said. "The killer didn't see you, but Nilla did."

"Your dog?" she scoffed.

"That's why she constantly barks and behaves erratically whenever she sees you. She was staring up at the balcony of this house overlooking my yard when we discovered Sabrina's body. No one except you and Nilla knew when she landed on the ground due to the loud music playing that night and you saw who pushed her."

She went to Debbie with desperation in her eyes. "Please make this woman leave. She's accusing me of something I have no knowledge of!"

Debbie lowered her head slightly. "I saw Nilla's reaction toward you the other day. She's always been a keen dog. Angela, look me in the eyes… did you see what happened to that young woman who died?"

Angela was quiet. To me, it was confirmation that my suspicions were correct.

"I am only an immigrant in this country," she said. "I have waited twelve years to be able to come here and have a good, decent life. I cannot be involved in any murder; I cannot take that chance. I don't want to be sent back."

Debbie took her hand and squeezed it gently. "They can't send you back for testifying as a witness to a murder. Your willingness to help convict the guilty party might actually help you to get permanent status here."

A load seemed to suddenly be lifted from Angela's face. "Are you sure?"

Debbie nodded. "I'm sure. Please tell us what you saw."

I finally took a seat while Angela explained what she'd witnessed from her employers' balcony that night. At the end, I made a phone call to Mickey Carey, who advised me to have Debbie bring Angela to his office right away where she'd make a sworn statement before he contacted the Sheriff—the only one he trusted in the Department.

Next, I rang Merlene's number. "Meet me at Mickey's office," I said. "I have something to tell you urgently."

Debbie, Angela and I headed to Mickey's office where Angela gave her statement and signed the affidavit. I handed over the print-out to Mickey from the phone company as well. His suspicions were just as good as mine concerning the number that belonged to dear, old Freddie.

Evidently, Mickey was having an easy run after all, for whatever his legal fees were about to be, considering I'd done just about all of the leg work.

Merlene arrived at the firm shortly after we did and I filled her in on everything.

"My goodness, Lucille! Why didn't you tell me you were doing any of this?" she said, as we sat alone. "You took it all on by yourself. I could've helped in some way."

"No. You had your hands full already. And furthermore, you would've only gotten in the way."

She managed a smile, then came over and gave me a great, big hug.

"You're the best friend a person could ever have. I can't express to you how grateful I am to call you not just my friend, but my *sister,*" she said.

That touched me. I always wanted a sister. For her to call me that, I guess was a good substitution for the fact that I never had a blood one.

We all waited for Sheriff Cooke to show up and in the end, a plan was set in motion that mostly involved *me*. Hopefully, if we pulled it off in a couple of days, David would be released and charges never filed against him.

18

"Why in the world is he still being held?" Merlene demanded an answer from Cooke as we stood inside his office. The place reeked of cigar smoke.

"I thought we went through this, Merlene! David's good with it; he understands what we're doing. What is it that you don't get?"

Cooke was clearly agitated. I had a hunch he hadn't tackled too many of these types of investigations and needed his focus to remain glued to the task at hand. Merlene was proving to be a distraction and I knew it wasn't a good thing.

"I don't trust you people!" she replied. "When this is over, I have a thing or two to say to you and your detectives."

"Okay, that's fine!" Cooke raised his hands. "Now, if you don't mind, we have to get a move on."

He looked at Theodore. "Are you ready, son?"

"Surely am," Theodore said.

"Well, get her there and then get out of the way like we discussed, okay?"

Theodore gave him a thumbs up.

I turned to Merlene. "Stay calm. Remember, this is for David's benefit; just keep that in mind, all right?" I spoke softly.

"All right." She nodded. "But I meant what I said."

"I know you did."

She remained behind with Cooke as Theodore and I headed out.

"Are you scared?" Theodore asked after we left the parking lot.

"Of who?" I pretended not to know.

"Of the people you're going to see."

"Why should I be scared? Okay... no, I'm not," I assured him.

It was a quarter past eleven, but already it seemed like I'd been awake for an entire day. I don't think I ever settled down since certain things were unraveled two days earlier. Anthony couldn't come along, but he was uptight about the whole matter; not feeling confident that I should've gotten so deeply involved in something he felt could backfire in the worst way. I never knew he cared about me so much and I was deeply touched.

Theodore pulled up in front of the main office of the Pichton Pet Society. I got out of the car and he saw me inside before pulling off.

The receptionist gave me an exceptionally warm welcome the moment I arrived and immediately took me to the conference room at the end of the hallway. Whomever the interior decorator was for the main offices of the compound deserved an award for creative excellence. The place looked rich with brown marble tiles both on the floors and midway up the walls, and the remaining section of the wall had been painted a light tannish color. A large flat screen TV had been braced to the wall in the conference room and tall, clear vases decked with colorful floral arrangements sat on round, glass side tables.

Recess lighting brightened the space and gave the room an exotic feel.

A few minutes later, Claire Fairweather entered the room with a smile stretched across her narrow face.

"Lucille, thanks for coming in! I must admit I was quite startled by your phone call. Can I offer you anything to drink?" She rested her briefcase and cell phone on the large, oval desk.

"Do you have champagne?"

"Um…sure. Sure, we do, and the finest, I might add."

She opened the door and summoned the receptionist. "Tamara, please bring two glasses of the finest champagne we have."

"Just two?" I asked. "Isn't your husband, Freddie, coming to join us and any of the other board members?"

"Unfortunately, no other board members are in, but Freddie is here. He usually oversees everything around the compound. I'll give him a call and ask him to run right over."

She picked up her cell and made the call, then she sat down on the opposite side of the table.

"This is so exciting, Lucille! How wonderful of you to offer to help out in such a grand way," she said.

"The pleasure is all mine."

The champagne arrived a few minutes later and I wasted no time indulging in its light, fruity essence. I realized it would've been proper for me to wait for dear Freddie so that we all could make a toast, but it wasn't every day I felt like being *proper*.

Freddie walked in and sat next to his wife. Although he tried to hide it, it was obvious that he did not want to be there. Maybe there was something about me that made the poor guy nervous or anxious, or whatever he was. His demeanor was cold and edgy and just being around the guy made me a bit perturbed.

"Mrs. Pfiffer…" He managed an even hail.

"Freddie…" I replied in like manner.

"Well, I'd like to propose a toast!" Claire was as prim as a peacock. "To Lucille Pfiffer for being an active, extraordinary member of the Pichton Pet Society!"

We all raised our glasses. The *modest me* would've shied away from such praise, but I never denied the fact that I do relish attention.

After we all took a collective sip of our champagne, I reached into my purse, retrieved a white envelope and placed it on the table in front of us. "This is for the society," I said. "I hope it will do a lot to save the animals out there."

Freddie picked it up and handed it to Claire. She immediately slid the check out of the envelope. "Twenty-five thousand dollars!" she said with pure delight twinkling in her eyes. “My goodness, Lucille! When you said this morning that you had a donation, I never imagined it would be so huge! Thank you so very much.” She was smiling from ear to ear and Freddie managed to crack a smile as well. “Isn’t this wonderful, dear?” she said to him.

“Yes, dear. It’s fantastic.”

He was gradually appearing more at ease.

“I’d better be on my way, but before I go, I must ask you a question. And to be quite frank with you, your answer depends on whether or not you’ll be able to cash that check.” Suddenly, a puzzled expression emerged on both of their faces as they glanced at each other.

“Okay…what is it, Lucille?” Claire asked.

“Remember the party at my house?”

“Uh huh.” She nodded. Freddie only stared.

“The one that was meant to celebrate my husband’s and my fiftieth wedding anniversary?”

“Yes…”

I could tell her curiosity was piqued.

“Well, which one of you tossed poor little Sabrina off my balcony?”

They glanced at each other again.

"What are you talking about?" Claire exclaimed.

I sighed deeply. "Let's be grown adults, shall we? We all know what it is I'm talking about." I leaned in. "Let me level with you. Hard evidence has been uncovered pertaining to what happened to Sabrina. I'm lucky to have come across it myself and haven't yet turned it over to the police. Let me add that it's in safekeeping, so if something, by chance, happens to me, it will automatically be found by the police and the guilty party promptly arrested." I paused just to take in the worried look on both of their faces. "That young lady didn't accidentally fall to her death; someone deliberately pushed her."

"You say you got evidence?" Freddie asked. Suddenly, he could speak!

"Yes... *hard* evidence—the kind that sticks to the bones," I said. "I'm prepared to keep whatever you say hush hush. I personally didn't like the girl; didn't think she was right for David and furthermore, I'm now a member of this honorable Society. If this is anything like the Templars, members here should never squeal on each other. It should be a real brother-sisterhood, you know? All for one—one for all."

Claire nodded. "I agree."

Freddie seemed a bit confused and distrusting.

"So, which one of you killed her?"

Claire turned to Freddie. "I guess you might as well tell her."

"Tell her what? I didn't kill that girl!" he replied.

"So, you only slept with her? That's all?" she returned.

He was suddenly quiet again.

"We've had this discussion time and time again, Freddie. You never stopped seeing her despite the times I told you to end it. That's why you were so nervous when she showed up that night at the party. You didn't expect her to be there, did you? And from the way she carried herself, she obviously didn't wanna be there either. Both of you looked so very uncomfortable, like you wanted to get the hell out of there. Did she finally walk away from you since you couldn't bring yourself to walk away from her? Is that what prompted you to sneak up to the room where she was at and get rid of her? Was it a case where if you couldn't have her, no one could?"

I was blown away by Claire's dramatic assertion and I could tell Freddie was just as shocked that she'd thrown him under the bus in front of a mere stranger.

"That's hogwash!" he replied. "I would've never killed her. I…"

"Loved her?" Claire proposed.

She sighed heavily, then turned to me. "There's no need not to involve the police in this matter, Lucille. The entire scenario has been laid out on the table for you. I'm not going down for a man who couldn't keep his weenie in his pants."

"Look, Lucille… I didn't do anything. She's talking out of her head," he asserted.

"I'm willing to testify against him," Claire continued. "I've got a lot of juicy news to tell the court."

I raised my chin slightly. "Why don't we start with the truth, Claire?"

She looked at me as if I had horns. "What are you talking about? I told you the truth!"

"If that's the truth, then I don't know what a lie is," I replied. Freddie looked at me curiously. "Let's stop the charade. Someone saw what you did to that girl."

"Nonsense!" Her eyes widened in defense.

"From the angle you were sitting at when you all were playing board games, you saw

David and Sabrina mount the stairs and noticed they both were angry or at least not on good terms. I excused myself and went upstairs to use the bathroom and when I returned to the living room, you were not there."

"So what? I went outside to take a breather. Is that against the law?"

"No. But murdering someone is."

"How dare you accuse me of murder, Lucille Pfiffer?"

Freddie was clearly surprised by the abrupt turn of events.

You saw David descend the staircase in a hurry and while I was up there, you snuck up yourself and stayed out of sight until you saw me leave. You then entered David's bedroom where Sabrina was and probably saw that she was still upset. To avoid a heated argument, you went there with one intention, and that was to settle the score. You perhaps pretended like you wanted to speak with her outside on the balcony where you'd have more privacy and she agreed, against her best judgment. You walked behind, allowing her to go out first. When she leaned against the rail, that's when you pushed her over. I presume you didn't even say another word to her before you did it."

Claire clapped her hands with a gleeful grin. "For a blind woman, you're pretty sharp."

"I'd take that as a compliment," I replied.

Freddie looked at his wife. "You mean… you did it? You killed her?"

"The word *kill* is such a strong word, dear. I kind of like took revenge. Yes, *revenge* is more appropriate."

He was glaring at her. "I can't believe it! And to think you were trying to blame me for her death just a few minutes ago."

"As far as I'm concerned, you're going to take the rap for it," she said. "Lucille here clearly has nothing in terms of evidence. She was just fishing for information and now she's got it. I, on the other hand, intend to turn you in and testify that I know, without a shadow of a doubt, that you killed poor Sabrina Abrams and asked me to cover it up, but I refused."

"Are you insane?" he said.

"Perhaps. I only could've been when I married you." She looked my way again. "Thanks again, Lucille, for your most generous donation and for protecting the interest of those in charge of running this most valuable operation. This twenty-five grand will go a long way."

That's when Sheriff Cooke, Detectives Lance Matthews and Tyrone Stewart entered the room. Several uniformed police officers and Merlene walked in behind them.

"What is this?" Claire rose to her feet and so did Freddie.

Cooke approached her. "You don't ask the questions here, lady. We do. Arrest her!"

The uniformed officers placed her under arrest.

Merlene hurried over and hugged me tightly.

"Good job, Lucille," Cooke said as I got up from the desk. "We managed to get everything on tape. For a moment there, I thought she'd never confess."

"I knew she would, eventually," I replied. "Narcissistic persons like herself revel in self-praise for a job well done—whether it was good or evil."

He nodded in agreement.

"I had nothing to do with any of it!" Freddie said in his defense.

"I know, buddy. You're free to go," Lance told him.

Freddie looked at his wife standing there in handcuffs, looking defeated. He sighed. "I'm not gonna turn my back on you like how you intended to do to me, Claire. Despite everything, I still love you."

"Even after how she tried to pin a murder on you?" Stewart asked, in disbelief.

"Even so." Freddie nodded.

"You've gotta be kidding!" Stewart shook his head.

There he was again, shooting that mouth off. I swear if I was a guy, I'd clobber him just to shut him up once and for all.

* * *

"You saved the day!" Merlene exclaimed as we were walking towards Theodore's car. "You saved David's life!"

Clutching the envelope with the check I'd given to Claire, I replied, "It was the least I could do for the boy. Hopefully, it'll make up for the last couple of birthday gifts I missed."

Merlene laughed. "By the way, they've released him."

"They have?" I replied, excitedly.

"Yes. He's right here."

"Where?"

He climbed out of Theodore's back seat, walked over and embraced me. "Thanks, Miss Lucille. I can't express how grateful I am for everything you've done for me. Without you, I probably would've rotted in jail."

My eyes welled with tears. "Like I told your mother, I hope it makes up for the last few birthday gifts I owe you."

He laughed as well. I guess they thought I was joking.

"Let's go home, everyone. Time to celebrate!" Theodore said.

David turned to his mother. "After we spend some time at Miss Lucille's place today, I was wondering if I can come back home."

Merlene's face lit up. "Sure, you can! It's your house too."

He grabbed his mother and squeezed her tightly. "I love you, Mom. Thanks for sticking by me."

Merlene was in tears now. "That's what moms are for."

I rode with Theodore while Merlene and David travelled together. When we pulled up to the front gate, I heard music coming from the house. Inside, a crowd of people, mostly friends and acquaintances of Merlene, Theodore and myself wearing party hats and blowing whistles, greeted us. Anthony, in his glory, had quickly arranged the whole thing. Debbie, Gary and Judy

Anderson were there and I later learned that blabbermouth Carla and a few other neighbors were not invited. That was fine by me. Mickey Carey and several of his associates were there too. Anthony expressed that it was a coming home celebration for David, but also a make-up anniversary party for Donnie and me. I couldn't believe he'd done that for us. Like I said, my boys are the best! I could've only hoped and prayed that day there was not about to be another murder on my property.

Sir Clement visited me that night and gave his nod of approval. I knew I never could've solved the mystery without him and did not forget to thank him. I also came to terms that he served a special purpose in my life, though I wasn't yet sure what that was. Maybe his own tragic ending truly had something to do with it. But the question remained: What was his connection to my inner vision and why did it now seem more stabilized since the murder? Did my willingness to help a friend and her son earn me brownie points? Perhaps, I'd learn more in the near future and maybe all my questions will be answered.

Nilla received an extra special doggie treat for the awesome part she played in unraveling the mystery surrounding Sabrina's death. I wondered if the little dog-shaped treat tasted like chocolate cake or butterscotch ice cream because the second she got it, she ran off to a corner of the room to privately savor it.

19

Merlene insisted on that meeting in the Sheriff's office the following day. Mickey and I were there for moral support. David wanted no part of the Sheriff's office ever again in life, so he declined his mother's invitation to join us.

Lance and Stewart sat on the same side of the desk as Cooke, while Mickey, Merlene and I faced them.

"Why did you use my son as a scapegoat," Merlene started, "when you already had documentation that clearly indicated Sabrina could've been seeing someone else? Why didn't you pursue the other person whose phone number was prevalent in her records apart from David's?

Cooke glanced at Lance, before addressing Merlene. "We didn't use David as a scapegoat, Merlene. We found the evidence against him stronger than any other party we came across."

"Sheriff, may I interject here?" Lance asked.

Cooke eagerly gave him the nod.

"I think I should put it out there that Frederick Fairweather's relationship or should I say, *connection* to Sabrina was being investigated…"

"While you were already holding David?" Mickey asked.

"Yes," Lance replied.

Mickey scoffed. "I find it odd that you're going to investigate the man after you've already arrested who you thought to be your prime suspect."

"We wanted to cover all our bases, Counselor."

"Come on! Let's be real here," Mickey retorted. "You refused to touch the Fairweathers because they were politically connected, particularly, Mrs. Fairweather."

"Then you should know we had to have all our bases covered and evidence in place before making any type of move," Lance said. "We were getting there."

"I don't think you were," Merlene countered. "Prosecuting David would've been much easier for you—even with the doubt, I'm sure you all had in your minds, of his guilt. You were just being lazy and wanted to take the easy route to close the case."

"That's not true, Merlene," Cooke said. "We were all working diligently to get to the bottom of this matter. Let me remind you that no charges were filed against David."

Merlene stood up. "No. Not yet. If Lucille hadn't come forward with something you couldn't shove underneath the rug—the housekeeper's testimony and the phone records that you guys were no longer the only ones privy to—you would've railroaded my David. Well, shame on you—all three of you knuckleheads!"

"No need for insults," Steward said, abruptly.

"Don't you tell me what's necessary! You didn't do what was necessary to arrest and convict the right person. I'm gonna tell you something and y'all had better listen well: You better hope history doesn't repeat itself, this time involving your own children, if you have any. I know *you* do, Sheriff. When you're out there handling other people's children, remember Sherry and Hank."

"There she goes threatening again!" Lance shook his head.

"I didn't perceive a threat," Mickey immediately replied.

"There's something called Karma," she continued. "In other words: What goes around comes around. You messed with my son; you put him through hell, but you'll face what you've done one way or the other. And I'll make it clear for the record. I'm not threatening to do anything to anyone. Whatever happens to any of you idiots in the future, you've done it to yourself."

Merlene helped me up, then said to Mickey, "That's all I wanted to say. Let's go."

* * *

That day, I officially resigned as member of the Pichton Pet Society. After what transpired concerning the Fairweathers, I figured I would've been kicked out if I hadn't resigned anyway. Thought I'd better protect my dignity. I decided to look into another reputable animal charity, even if it wasn't locally based or I'd start my own someday. I never tore up that check I wrote to the Society. Instead, I kept it as a reminder of how associating with snobbish people can ultimately bring murder to your doorstep. Hopefully, I would've learned my lesson.

I'm glad to say with Angela's testimony and Claire's secretly recorded confession, the

Pichton Pet Society Chairperson and Lecturer at our local college was sentenced to life with the possibility of parole in twenty-five years. By then, she'd be around eighty years old. I doubt she'd be a threat to anyone. But you never know…

As you can see, when I joined the local pet society, I never dreamed that shortly thereafter, I'd be involved in a murder investigation. I'll never forget that first meeting, those well-to-do people, and the questions they asked. To me, my being there was just something to do for the welfare of animals, but it turned out to be so much more—so much worse than I could've imagined.

~ The End ~

~ Keep reading to see what's coming next in this exciting, new series! ~

*** Will Lucille learn the real reason for Sir Clement's visits and that of the others?

*** Will her disclosure of the half a million insurance dollar payout be kept confidential by her best friend, Merlene?

BLIND ESCAPE - Book 2 in The Lucille Pfiffer Mystery Series

The town of Chadsworth has a new headache on its hand...a puzzling murder for blind Lucille Pfiffer to solve. Will the mystery be unraveled in record time or will the stealthy killer or killers find their way to Lucille's doorstep?

Her dog, Vanilla, once again claims her role as "protector". But Lucille is majorly concerned—not just for her own safety, but for that of her cherished pet.

An exciting, new mystery series is here!

GET BOOK 2 IN THIS EXCITING, NEW COZY MYSTERY SERIES!

***** Loving this series? Keep reading for your free excerpt of BOOK ONE of my 5 star rated Cornelius series! *****

CORNELIUS (Book 1 of The Cornelius Saga)

~ #1 bestseller ~

FREE EXCERPT

PROLOGUE

It was a day and age much like today where every town, generation and household held firmly its secrets—torrid improprieties they would protect to the end of the world. Yet some secrets back then were far too shocking and disturbing to contain—ones entangled with emotions of such intensity that would shock the very life out of 'innocent', reserved folk.

The year was 1861. The town of Mizpah was on the verge of the abolition of slavery. White people with a conscience and black folk alike prayed and fought long and hard for the day when all human beings were considered equal in the eyes of the law.

Cornelius Ferguson, only the wealthiest planter in all of Mizpah, didn't support the views of the abolitionist movement in that territory nor in any other for that matter. Negro labor was highly favorable for his pockets and he couldn't imagine conducting his plantation affairs by any other means.

June 12th of 1861 was the day his life would forever change. It was the day a colored girl by the name of Karlen Key walked through his door. She was beautiful, literate, well-spoken—a rare breed and long-awaited trade off from another planter across the river. Cornelius had been anticipating her arrival. Germina, a rotund, elderly house slave with a few long strands protruding from her chin, met Karlen at the door and showed her where to put her tattered bag. Cornelius stood thirty feet away in the great room facing the entrance way, highly pleased and mesmerized by the new addition to his household. Karlen's eyes met his for a brief moment before she quickly lowered her head, made a slight bow and greeted her master. The twenty-one-year-old had no idea that her arrival at the Ferguson plantation would alter the course of her life and those around her in a most uncanny way.

1

Summer of 1965

"Wade! Mira!" Sara Cullen called her kids from outside the kitchen door. "Time to come inside and get yourselves cleaned up for dinner!"

Fourteen-year-old, Wade and thirteen-year-old, Mira were in the road playing 'bat and ball' in front of their yard with Monique Constantakis and her cousin Philip. Mira had just swung the bat for her turn to run the bases.

"Let's go!" Wade shouted to his sister as she considered one last run before heading inside. "If you don't come now, I'm leaving you and you'll be in big trouble with Dad." On that, he took off up to the driveway of their home and Mira, with a tinge of disappointment, handed the bedraggled, semi-splintered bat to Monique who was standing behind her.

"See you later," Monique said, visibly disappointed that her new friend had to leave.

"Yeah," Mira said before heading up the driveway behind her brother who had disappeared into the house.

The table, as usual, had been beautifully set for dinner. Sara Cullen was a true perfectionist and wanted everything to be just right when her husband of fifteen years, Michael, stepped into the dining room for his meal. She worshipped the dirt the man walked on and kept herself in the finest physical shape she could possibly manage. She was five feet, ten inches tall, and remarkably thin. Her hair was long, black and curly, and her features narrow. Michael Cullen was not the most attractive man in the world, but he carried big, broad shoulders and a six-pack most men would die for. Furthermore, he collected a handsome paycheck at the end of each week, lived in a nice neighborhood, and sported a two-year-old red Jaguar. Nevertheless, Sara—Head Nurse at Freedom Hospital—could not be accused of being with him solely for his money or his executive status at the State-run Gaming Board. They had met fresh out of high school when all they had ahead of them were nothing more than dreams and aspirations.

Mira sat at the table first though Wade had been the first to wash up.

"Wade! Where are you?!" Sara cried, as she hurried around placing the remaining items on the table. The boy showed up moments later.

"Where were you all that time?" Sara asked. "You know I like both of you to be seated before I call your dad out."

"I had to… brush my hair." Wade lowered his head slightly.

"That's a lie!" Mira blurted with a wide smile. "He had to use the toilet!"

"Liar!" Wade rebutted.

"You had to use the toilet! You had to use the toilet!" Mira sang.

"Now stop it - both of you!" Sara barked. "This is no time for games... and wipe that smile off your face Mira; I'm not playing!"

"Yes, Mother," Mira softly replied.

The children composed themselves and waited patiently for their father who emerged a few minutes later from the master bedroom.

"Kids…" Michael hailed straight-faced as he sat down.

Both children responded monotonically, "Hi, Dad."

Sara joined them moments later.

As was customary for the family, they all bowed their heads at the sound of Michael's utterance, "Let us pray" before diving into their meals.

From her chair, Mira watched as her mother talked and talked to her father while he engaged very little in the conversation. It was like that all the time and Mira was beginning to wonder why her mother even tried. What Sara saw in Michael that was so appealing and attractive totally eluded Mira. Michael was a brutally rigid man who, in his daughter's opinion, always seemed to wish he was somewhere else other than at home.

"May I be excused?" Mira asked fifteen minutes later, wanting to escape the drab, depressive atmosphere of the room.

"But you hardly touched your casserole," Sara said, noticing for the first time that her daughter had barely eaten.

"I'm not hungry."

"Are you all right, honey?" Sara asked, as Michael continued his meal supposedly unaffected.

"Yes, Mom. I just feel a bit tired and would like to lie down," Mira replied.

"You may leave," Michael said, not making eye contact.

"Well then…" Sara continued, "I'll cover your plate for you in case you get hungry before bedtime."

"Thanks Mom." Mira backed out from the table and retreated to her bedroom.

Approximately a half hour later, there was a light tap at the bedroom door. The doorknob turned slowly, then Sara walked in. "Are you all right?" She asked Mira who was curled up in bed with a Sherlock Holmes mystery.

"Sure." Mira sat up as her mother proceeded to the side of the bed.

She felt her daughter's forehead with the back of her hand. "No fever. That's good. Are you sure you're okay?" The look she gave was a combination of suspicion and concern.

"Yes. I'm really fine, Mom. I just wasn't hungry; that's all—I guess from all that running around earlier."

"I see." Sara got up. "Well, like I said… if you get hungry later, your food is right there covered in the refrigerator. Wouldn't want you going to bed empty only to wake up all gassy in the morning."

Mira smiled. Her mother reached down and kissed her on the forehead. "I love you, sweet pea."

"I love you too, Mom."

2

"You wanna go by the canal today?" Wade asked Mira at the kitchen counter. An early riser, he had been up for well over an hour, but she had just gotten out of bed.

"Dad said we can't go back there—you know that," Mira answered, cracking an egg over a bowl.

"He's not here. Mom's not here. They don't have to know," Wade replied. "We can get our fishing rods, some bait, and maybe this time, we'll actually catch something."

"I don't know… the last time we got caught out there we almost got a good whipping. Dad's hand was itching. Luckily, he let us off the hook with a warning. Off the hook… got it?"

"Look! They're both at work. We'll only be gone for a few hours and will be back long before they get here. They'll never know, so we're not risking anything." Wade was adamant.

"I don't know, Wade," Mira said, pouring a little cream into the bowl with her egg.

"Why are you so scared?" Wade asked. "We've been to the canal dozens of times and only got caught that one time when dad pulled up out of nowhere. You think he's gonna drive all the way home from work today on a sneaky suspicion that we're at the canal again and bust us for not listening? Come on, Mira!"

"Okay, okay. We can go after I've had my breakfast. I suppose you've eaten already?" Mira asked.

"Yeah. I'm cool. I'll go pack the gear."

The canal was less than a block away. It usually took the kids a mere four minute walk to get there. Mira, dressed in a yellow and white striped blouse and red shorts walked quickly behind her brother, inwardly hoping and praying that their father would not pull up and surprise them while they were on the way to the 'forbidden place'.

"We need to walk faster," Mira said, now over-taking her brother. Wade silently caught up with her and in no time, they were at their favorite spot.

The canal was the only one in their neighborhood. It extended miles out to the sea. Several gated houses with boat decks surrounded it, except for a fifty-foot open area that was partially clear due to low, sparse bushes and a padded, gravel area kept in check by occasional vehicles driving through.

Mira sat down at the edge of the canal, her feet dangling against its rocky structure. Wade got the fishing rods ready before sitting next to her. He handed Mira a rod with bait attached and threw his out into the not-so-shallow water. For a while, they just sat there looking out into the water at tiny schools of fish swimming around.

"What's on your mind?" Wade asked, still looking straight ahead.

"What do you mean?" Mira glanced at him.

"You're so quiet. What're you thinking about?"

"Nothing."

"You're the one lying now," Wade said.

"How can you say that I'm lying? Are you inside my brain, Wade Cullen?" Mira returned feistily.

"It's Mom and Dad, isn't it?"

Mira looked at him. "How do you know?"

"I know what's been going on. I can see it was getting to you. That's why you left the table yesterday, right?"

For a few moments, there was silence, then Mira finally answered: "I don't understand why Mom tries so hard to please Dad. It's not like he shows her he appreciates anything she does anyway."

"We've never known Dad to be a talkative person, Mira. He doesn't say much to us neither," Wade replied.

Again… there were a few moments of silence.

"I think his actions go beyond not being much of a talker, Wade. Dad can be so cold at times. I feel so bad for Mom when I see her trying so hard to please him all the time and he doesn't seem to be giving anything back to her. It's like she's in a relationship all by herself."

"Mom's used to Dad. They're just different people. She doesn't seem to mind when she's talking to him and it's obvious that he's not even listening. If she's not bothered by it, why should you let it bother you?"

"Because she's our mother, Wade. That's why. She deserves better than that," Mira answered.

"Better than Dad?"

"I think so."

Wade was shocked that his sister's feelings about the matter were that intense.

"What are you trying to say, Mira—that Dad's not good enough for Mom? Don't you love him?"

"Sure I do. I love them both, but I can tell that Mom's not happy. She pretends that she is because she lives in this 'perfect world' that she's created in her head."

Wade's eyes were on the water again. "I think I feel something..." he said moments later. "Yes! I got a bite!" He reeled in the rod as quickly as he could while Mira's eyes beamed at the prospect of him making a good catch. By then, they were both standing and watching an average-sized snapper wiggle its streamlined body on the hook.

"Yay! We got one!" Mira exclaimed.

Wade unhooked the fish and dumped it into their mother's mini cooler.

"That's a good one," Mira said, watching the fish flop around in the cooler.

"Yeah. Let's see if we can catch anymore."

They both sat back down and re-tossed their fishing rods after Wade baited his again.

A half hour passed and there was nothing. Wade could now sense Mira's restlessness. "You wanna wait a little while longer to see if we'll get another bite?" He asked.

"Na. Let's not push our luck," Mira said. "We got a fish. Let's go fry it."

After turning onto their street, Mira's eyes hit the large property straight ahead at the end of the corner. "You wanna go see if any dillies are on the trees? We can eat them with our fish," she said excitedly.

"The Ferguson property?" Wade asked.

"Yeah."

Since they would have to go past their house in order to get there, Wade said, "Okay. Let me take the cooler inside first."

Mira waited in the western side of the yard that was adjacent to the road. She was so relieved that the canal trip went well and was eager to season and fry the fish they had caught.

"Let's go," Wade appeared a minute later with an empty, plastic bag balled up in his hand. "Wanna race there?"

"Sure. Now!" Mira took off on her brother unexpectedly and knowing he had been duped, Wade ran with all his might to try and catch up to her. Mira had almost made it first to the edge of the Ferguson property before Wade's long legs finally caught up to her and overtook her. He was going so fast that he could barely cut his speed sufficiently before nearly slamming into the huge coconut tree directly in front of him. Mira laughed as she panted to catch her breath.

"You cheater!" Wade said after slumping under the tree.

"Don't blame me if I almost beat you here," Mira replied. "You always boast about being able to run faster than I can."

"Are you serious?!" Wade was flabbergasted. "I *can* run faster than you! Didn't I prove it again just now—even though you cheated, you little pipsqueak?!"

Mira advanced onto the large acreage and looked up at the dillies hanging temptingly from the large, outstretched tree branches of one of many trees that clustered the property. The Ferguson estate was comprised of approximately sixty acres of land which took up most of the road east to west, extending northwardly to the edge of another neighborhood. Wade and Mira had not walked even a good two acres of the land since they were old enough to 'explore'.

"This one's packed. You wanna climb?" Mira asked her brother. Wade was the official tree-climber of the pair since Mira was terrified of heights.

Wade got up off the ground holding his back like a man far beyond his years. "Okay.

You know the drill," he said, handing her the bag.

As Wade climbed the tree, Mira readied the bag so that he could drop the dillies into it. In seconds, he was at arm's length from the nearest tree branch. It was laden with mostly semi-ripe dillies. "I'm gonna start dropping now!" He cried.

Mira opened the bag as widely as possible and positioned herself directly under her brother as he dropped the fruit one by one. As usual, the bag had missed a few of them and Mira was bending down picking up the ones that had fallen without bursting on impact.

"You can't run and you can't catch!" Wade laughed in the tree as he deliberately dropped some of the dillies while she was still stooping down to pick up the others.

"You're stupid for dropping them, Wade. You're really immature!" She snarled.

Deciding they had enough of them, Wade came down from the tree and snatched one of the dillies out of the bag. As he ate, he looked around at the large property and an idea struck him. "How about we explore this land? We've never gotten further than just a few feet in everytime we come here."

"This is private property, Wade. We can't just go exploring," Mira replied, thinking how *slow* her brother really was. After all, the large, lop-sided NO TRESPASSING sign sprayed in red was clearly visible on the fence.

"You're gonna let an old NO TRESPASSING sign stop you from walking through here? Have you ever seen the owners out here? Have you ever seen *anyone* out here?"

Mira was quiet.

"Right! That's because no one ever comes here. The place is abandoned. What's wrong with a couple of kids just walking through a vacant property with a bunch of tall trees and bushes on it? What can we possibly do to hurt the land?" Wade said sarcastically. "Come on, Sis. It'll be fun. We can pretend that we're real explorers or something."

Mira was hesitant whenever Wade presented ideas that could possibly get them into trouble. Then again… those types of ideas were the only ones he ever seemed to come up with. "What about the fish?"

"What about it?" Wade was puzzled.

"We have to fry it before Dad and Mom gets back home."

Wade looked at Mira in disbelief. "Why are you so darn scary, girl? How long do you think they've been gone? It's only been a few hours. Last I knew, they got off work in the evening and then there's traffic. It's barely noon yet."

"How do you know what time it is?" Mira asked. "You don't have a watch."

"I can estimate the time, Mira. Can't you, smarty pants?"

Mira shoved the bag of fruit at him. "Here then! You carry this." And she slowly headed out into the wooded area.

As they walked along a narrow trail, the children were fascinated by the size of the property. Trees of every kind imaginable seemed to inhabit it—pine, mangoes, bananas, avocadoes, plum, ginep. Wade and Mira stopped and picked what they wanted, adding them to the bag, and the apprehension Mira had initially felt about their so-called exploration had soon disappeared.

"This is great," she said sucking on a plum.

"Awesome!" Wade agreed. "I feel like we're in the jungle or something. How long do you think it'll take us to walk the whole perimeter?"

Mira looked at him incredulously. "Are you out of your mind?" Do you think I'm gonna walk this entire property? I hear the Fergusons' land is more than a few miles long."

"I didn't mean we should walk the whole thing today. I was asking how long you think it would take us if we decided to," Wade explained.

"I don't know… maybe an hour or two." Then her eyes were suddenly affixed to a large house that they never knew was there. "Hey, look there!" Mira pointed straight ahead.

"Wow! That's huge!" Wade exclaimed, almost in slow motion. With heightened curiosity, he started running toward it.

"Wait up!" Mira shouted, careful to do so in a lowered voice as she had no idea who or what might be inside. "Don't go in there without me!"

However, old and dilapidated with broken windows showcased along the whole front view, the house was breathtaking.

Wade climbed the colonial-style porch, stopping just about a foot away from the front door. The only thing is… there was no door—just a ten foot opening where there, most likely, used to be double doors.

Wade looked inside. Grimy white tiles covered the entire front area as far as he could see.

Mira climbed the porch moments later. "Do you see anything?" She asked softly, feeling a bit of apprehension gradually returning.

"No," Wade whispered. "Is anyone in here?" He called out hoping not to receive an answer.

They stood quietly, both decidedly ready to take off in an instant if they heard even a crack. They waited for a few seconds… nothing. Then Wade said, in not so much of a whisper anymore, "Let's go in."

Mira grasped his arm. He was just eleven months older than she was, but in a case like that where they were entering the *unknown*, he could have very well been ten years older and fifty pounds heavier as she knew 'come hell or high water', he would protect her.

Before stepping inside, Wade looked at her, "You mind letting up a bit? You're squeezing my arm."

"Oh sorry," Mira replied nervously.

They walked inside together—eyes darting in all directions of the spacious interior. The white paint on the wall was chipped in several places and the dusty floor had been speckled with creature droppings and smudges of dirt and mud. There was no furniture in sight—just a large, empty space. Wade and Mira walked slowly ahead and entered a room that looked like an extension of the living room, only separated by an arched wall.

"Hello…" Wade called out again.

"Is anyone here?" Mira said behind him, voice breaking at the end.

They proceeded through the large front area then entered what looked like the kitchen. There was one row of cabinets still attached to the upper northern section of the wall with a few missing doors. Some doors were slanted due to rusty, broken hinges. There were three other sections of the wall where only the imprint of cabinets remained presenting a theory to the observer that they might have been cleanly extracted at some point by thieves.

"This place is a mess," Mira uttered, still holding her brother's arm.

"Yeah. You notice that just about every door around here is missing?"

"Yeah."

"Let's go upstairs," Wade released Mira's grip. "Follow me."

"No way! You know I'm afraid of heights!" Mira whispered loudly.

"Just hold on to the rail. You'll be fine," Wade replied before heading up the long winding staircase.

Feeling that she would rather be with him than downstairs alone in the old, creepy house that resembled something from a horror flick, she took a deep breath in and decided to follow him. The ceiling of the house was extremely tall and as Mira carefully followed Wade up the stairs, she couldn't help but wonder how the owners ever managed to change a light bulb up there whenever necessary. As they climbed the staircase, the wood beneath their feet creaked and Mira had no idea how she would ever get back down.

They made it to the second landing and refusing at that point to look down over the rail, Mira trailed closely behind Wade who had entered one of the bedrooms.

"Wow! This room is huge!" Wade remarked, hurrying over to a large window on the western side of the room. "Hee, hee!" He laughed looking down at the yard. "The second floor of this house must be at least a hundred feet from the ground!"

Mira quietly advanced toward the entrance of what looked like the walk-in closet. As she looked in, something immediately caught her eye. The floating image of a black woman was at the far end of the room. The apparition appeared relatively young with frazzled, black hair that hung tiredly just above her shoulders. Her face, rough and haggard, exuded a sadness that Mira could feel deep within her bones, and the thin, white dress the woman wore was drenched in what appeared to be blood around the mid-section where long trails of it had slid down to the end. Momentarily frozen by the sight of this woman, Mira's mouth hung open, yet no voice escaped. The woman's veiny eyes seemed to be begging, pleading… for something. Then her hand reached up toward Mira, re-enforcing what the little girl already felt was a cry for help. At that point, a blood-curdling scream escaped Mira's lungs and she darted outside of the room—Wade running behind her.

With a fear of heights that paled in comparison to what she saw in that room, before Mira knew it, she was at the bottom of the staircase and out of the house.

"What's wrong?" Wade called out to her in the yard. "Wait for me, Mira!"

She had run a good distance away from the house before even thinking of stopping.

"Tell me what's wrong!" Wade insisted after catching up to her. "I never saw you run that fast in my life."

"I know I shouldn't have listened to you, Wade. You're a jerk! We never should have come here," Mira blasted, walking hurriedly.

"What did *I* do?" Wade was confused.

"I don't wanna talk about it right now. I just wanna go home."

While darting out of the house, Wade had dropped the bag of fruits they had collected. The children walked home together without saying another word. Wade knew that he had to get to the bottom of what happened in that house; Mira was not going to fold up on him as she sometimes did. After all, he felt responsible for her and now guilty that she had been so traumatized by something that in spite of her fear of heights, she had run down a tall flight of stairs without giving it a second thought.

After arriving home, Mira went straight to her room and slammed the door. Wade went to the door and knocked lightly. "Mira… what happened back there?" He tried to turn the doorknob, but discovered it was locked. "Open up. I wanna talk to you."

"Go away!" Mira yelled.

With head hung low and feeling worse by the second, Wade asked: "What about the fish? Aren't we gonna fry it before Mom and Dad get back?"

"I don't care. Do what you want with it!" Mira replied.

"Why do you have to be like this? Why can't you just tell me what happened, Mira? You say I'm immature, but you're the immature one!"

Wade waited for a response, but didn't get one, so he went into the kitchen to prepare the fish. After scaling and seasoning their catch, he walked around to the side of the house, made an outdoor fire like he and Mira had done so many times and placed a tin frying pan on top of the heap. As the oil heated inside the pan, Wade sat on one of the two large rocks close by, elbow under chin, thinking of how good their day had been and how it ended up. He felt terrible for Mira and wished she didn't get in those quiet moods sometimes, thus closing herself off to the world. She didn't realize that whenever she did that, he felt completely lost.

After the oil came to a slight boil, he put the fish in the pan and watched as swarms of flies suddenly appeared out of nowhere around it. Shooing them away, Wade refused to go inside and cook on the stove: He and Mira had established something special together out there frying their catch on the make-shift stove and no army of flies was going to change that.

After turning the fish over with a spatula, Wade looked up and saw Mira approaching. She went and sat down on the other large rock near the fire. Wade, elated that his sister had decided to join him, showed no reaction.

"The fish looks good," Mira said, looking at her brother.

Unable to hold back any longer, Wade asked: "What happened in that house, Mira? Why did you leave like that?"

Mira looked down for a moment. "I'm not sure. I thought… I saw something."

"Saw what?" Wade probed, curiosity in over-drive.

"I saw a woman, okay?" Mira decided to just get it out in spite of how crazy it might sound. "She was wearing a long, white dress—looked old fashioned to me—and it was covered in blood."

Wade gawked. "Are you serious?"

"'Course, I'm serious!" Mira snapped. "You think I would've took off like that for nothing?"

"Where was she?"

"In the closet."

"What was she doing?"

"Just standing there," Mira replied. "She seemed so sad. Well, I'm not going back there anymore. I don't care about dillies or anything else. I'm never going back on that property."

"I wonder why she's there." Wade was engrossed in thought.

"So you believe me?" Mira asked, feeling hopeful.

"Sure, I do. I know you'd never make something like that up. Besides, from the way you took off down those stairs, you had to see something." He laughed.

Mira smiled, then laughed out loud. Wade jumped on that opportunity to tease her as they sat and waited for their fish to cook.

VISIT TANYA-R-TAYLOR.COM TO KEEP READING *CORNELIUS*

OR GET THE FIRST **10 BOOKS** IN THE BEST SELLING CORNELIUS SAGA SERIES!

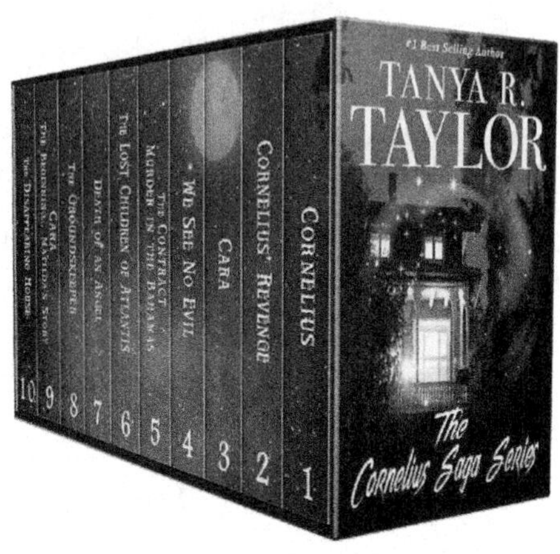

Never Miss a New Release by
Tanya R. Taylor!

Sign up at
Tanya-r-taylor.com

Other Fiction Titles by Tanya R. Taylor

Visit Tanya's website

TANYA-R-TAYLOR.COM

INFESTATION: A Small Town Nightmare (The Complete Series)
Real Illusions: The Awakening
Real Illusions II: REBIRTH
Real Illusions III: BONE OF MY BONE
Real Illusions IV: WAR ZONE
Cornelius (Book 1 in the Cornelius saga. *Each book in this series can stand-alone.*)
Cornelius' Revenge (Book 2 in the Cornelius saga)
CARA: Some Children Keep Terrible Secrets (Book 3 in the Cornelius saga)
We See No Evil (Book 4 in the Cornelius saga)
The Contract: Murder in The Bahamas (Book 5 in the Cornelius saga)
The Lost Children of Atlantis (Book 6 in the Cornelius saga)
Death of an Angel (Book 7 in the Cornelius saga)
The Groundskeeper (Book 8 in the Cornelius saga)
Haunted Cruise: The Shakedown

The Haunting of MERCI HOSPITAL
Hidden Sins Revealed (A Crime Thriller - Nick Myers Series Book 1)
One Dead Politician (Nick Myers Series Book 2)
10 Minutes before Sleeping

Made in the USA
Middletown, DE
07 July 2020